Near-Life Experiences

For Jack,
with best
wishes,

Near-Life Experiences

THE BEST OF JON CARROLL

by Jon Carroll

FOREWORD BY ANNE LAMOTT

CHRONICLE BOOKS • SAN FRANCISCO

Printed in the USA.

Library of Congress Cataloging in Publication Data

Carroll, Jon
Near-Life Experiences: the best of Jon Carroll/by Jon Carroll:
introduction by Anne Lamott.
p. cm.
A collection of 100 of the author's columns, revised by the author,
selected from the San Francisco Chronicle.
ISBN 0-8118-0307-4 (pbk.)
I. Title
PN4877.C32 1993
814'.54—dc20

92-280
CIP

Book and cover design © Adrian Morgan at Red Letter Design

Distributed in Canada by Raincoast Books
112 East Third Ave., Vancouver, B.C. V5T 1C8

10 9 8 7 6 5 4 3 2 1

Chronicle Books
275 Fifth Street
San Francisco, CA 94103

For Tracy,
Old Knots Just Get Stronger

Table of Contents

Foreword by Anne Lamott

Day after day for the last ten years in *The San Francisco Chronicle*, Jon Carroll has turned his quirky intelligence to the whole range of things that make up life in the modern world, from shopping for pants to world peace and abortion; from sports and clowns and gardens to the deep romantic love he feels for his wife; from raising children and getting older to cats, and hair loss, and poverty. He expresses political outrage as eloquently as anyone writing today. Here is someone who against all odds has not given up on the ideals of justice and freedom and mercy for all people. (The guy must be some kind of a nut.) Here is a writer who can make you laugh so hard that you begin making honking sounds, and yet who can also express the fragility and vulnerability of human life, the tenderness of the human heart. Here is a person who, behind the sometimes soaring rhythms of the prose, the wild imagination and wit, the dead-on accuracy of the satire and jibes and sarcasm, the outraged complaints, the good-natured confusion, the fury at injustice, holds to a simple belief that people are smart, and can be trusted, and should be loved.

Carroll is able to write about anything; for instance, the joy of snorkeling:

"My theory about why everyone in the entire world does not snorkel as often as possible has to do with its name: snorkel. Snorkel sounds like hunting for truffles; it sounds like something your doctor would ask you to do if he wanted to check your sinuses. 'Just turn your head and snorkel for me, Mr. Carstairs.'"

He writes about the homeless, about the rich, about being at an extravagant party at the Getty Mansion, looking for a bathroom, and being told, "Go up the stairs, and take a left at the maid." He loves his garden, and in it, he flourishes in a kind of crabby, befuddled way:

"I am digging in the earth. My hands are cold; my knees are sore; my back is sending me brisk telegrams: 'Don't Try To Stand Up Stop I Am Locked In This Position Forever Stop Please Stop Stop.' And yet I continue. Beside me, in a limp cardboard box, are a large number of small brown objects. They look like onions rejected by sensible shoppers, or worse. Chimpanzee leavings. Gnome scat. Bulbs. I am placing these bulbs in the ground . . . ."

Over and over, in a wide range of styles and tones, he gives us those two great gifts of telling the truth and of making us laugh at ourselves and at our world, so that we can dance with the frequent absurdity of life instead of being squashed by it.

In an era when most wit has a manufactured television quality, Carroll's has literary roots, a storyteller's joy, a delight in words. He makes us laugh out loud early in the morning (which is no small feat) provoking smiles and chuckles and sometimes the free falls of recognition. Listen for a moment to "I Think I'm Losing My Whatchamacallit":

"I first realized that I was losing vital brain functions when . . . well, I can't remember the first time I realized it. I think it was right around that big holiday in September, the picnic one. You know. It was right around that picnic holiday we were with Fred and Fred's wife, Una. Not Una, Edith? Can that be right? Starts with a vowel, though. Irene? Doesn't matter. We were eating dinner at that place right behind the place where the symphony plays. I remember it clearly because it was the first time I had that fish with the funny name. Orange something. The fish itself was not actually orange. I remember noticing that. Orange roughneck. That can't be right. Came on a plate. Well, of course it came on a plate. Ha ha. So we were with Fred and Utne at that doodah restaurant, two syllables, and Fred said to me, 'In your new glasses, you look just

like . . . .' Now I can't remember. That Russian guy . . . ."

You find yourself laughing all the way through, sometimes out loud. But when you finish laughing, what you are left with is a sense of tenderness, for our species, for our condition, for how hard we try. And, you are left with a sense of hope.

"Hope is an obligation," I remember hearing him say, or else it was in one of his columns (see "I Think I'm Losing My Whatchamacallit" above), and this sense of hope shines through all his pieces. "Things are indeed terrible all over," one of his famous columns ends. "This is a known fact. What is not generally acknowledged is that things are also not terrible all over, that joy is just as real as death, and as easily available." There is hope all over the place, and there is selflessness, he insists, if you just look around, and there is grace. He is continually amazed by the presence of grace in the world, in the mountains, in our homes, in the garden, in ordinary people doing heroic things. In one column, for instance, we find him at San Francisco General, taking part in a memorial service for those who died at the hospital that month, many of them homeless and derelict, many of them friendless, foreigners, strangers in a strange land, being remembered only by the pastor and four or five people, regular clunky old people like ourselves who have just *shown up* to honor these people who did not live in good houses or die well. He is there for us all the way through this simple, tiny service. It is very quiet, and you hang on every word. "Then we began to sing the hymn," he writes, "not well but not too badly, and then we finished . . . . There was a small change in the room. It was as though a cup, balanced precariously on a windowsill, had been carried over to the center of the table."

Over and over again he writes of people who just happened to notice another of the small miracles, whether it occurred on a tropical island, or in the kitchen with his daughters, or even in the political arena. He has often mentioned a picture of the Buddha he saw once, with these words written underneath: "You must be present to win." This seems to be very much at the center of his rather chagrined and black-humored sense of the spiritual in everyday life. He seems to honestly believe the great clichés, that seeing is forgetting the names of things, that God is in the details, and that those who are not busy living are busy dying—but he'd never just come out and say so. He shows us, convinces us all over again, by standing in for us in foreign countries, and at political conventions, at graduations and floods, and funerals and circuses, by standing there, and *seeing*. And what he sees is the impossible beauty and the impossible violence and the sheer mystical sensuality of nature and all the living and dying and flowering and decaying and rising up once again that is life, that is in fact who we are.

Those of us who are entirely sold on Jon Carroll have spent too many years Xeroxing and mailing our favorite columns to one another. Now, because of this collection, we won't have to do so again for awhile. If you're new to the columns, we think you'll be amazed, that here is someone who *in a newspaper* actually writes about joy and wonder and romantic love, all the while avoiding Hallmark card clichés, staying instead in real life where things are so often drab or crazy and messy and time-consuming and transitory, and wherein we find all that is real and of value, all that endures. Reading these columns, we believe you will hear the many voices of a very, very funny man with a deep and abiding sense of humanity, who keeps reminding us that our earth is a lovely and ridiculous and fragile and tough and infinitely moving place to live, and that if you do show up and reject cynicism and pay attention, you will find yourself in the presence of the truly mind-boggling; who reminds us, again and again, that miracles so often come in plain brown wrappers.

Introduction

There have been no books written on how to be a columnist; there are no seminars on the subject. It's a sort of Outward Bound program for journalists; you're dropped into the middle of the wilderness with two pounds of coffee and a surly copy editor, and you're told to produce 800 words by 4 P.M. that very day. Then someone who controls your salary reads the words, and either you die or you don't.

Then you do it again the next day, and the next, and pretty soon you have 23,000 columns and a vague sense of having taken a journey, which is odd because the scenery hasn't changed.

When I got the job at *The Chronicle*—write five columns a week until we tell you to stop—Art Hoppe took me out to lunch as a comradely gesture. I asked him if he had any tips and he said he didn't, and we fell to complaining about management.

Steve Rubenstein took me out to lunch too, and he asked me for tips before I could ask him. So we fell to complaining about management.

Herb Caen provided an example: Work like hell. I rejected that option.

Herb is burdened by facts, and the necessity for checking the same. I decided early on that the fact, qua fact, would not play an enormous role in my column. There are so many facts and factlike particles in the newspaper already; why should I add to the load? If I get a fact, I try to make a whole column out of it.

I

The only idea I had when I started the job is that a newspaper column is rather more intimate an undertaking than is generally supposed. The essential interchange often takes place in the kitchen or the bathroom; no one is wearing a tie or eating canapes. Consistency of tone or topic is not a virtue; company manners are not required. Every day is a new beginning, a new voice.

So the column feels a lot like the inside of my own head: sarcastic and generous by turns, fascinated by trivia, unfair, contradictory, sentimental, vague, irritable, eager to please. Sometimes I have no idea what I think about something until I start writing about it; occasionally I have no idea what I've said until after I read it in print. I go with my instincts not because I think they're reliable, but because I have nothing else to go on.

I was 38 when I started the column, settling into middle age; I figured I had become whatever I was going to become, and I might as well just write whatever the hell I wanted. This has irritated any number of people, but one of the givens of the job is that I wake up every weekday morning with the certain knowledge that 50,000 people think I'm a jerk.

When in doubt, I write about sex or death. That sounds like a joke, and it is, but also it isn't.

I've spent all but one year of my life in California; for better or worse, the column is a California column. Californians have little self-consciousness about who they are, few aphorisms about their sense of place, but being from the left coast is as distinct a thing as being from Brooklyn. Sometimes I get touchie-feelie; sometimes I get overenthusiastic. It's our way out here; we're still pretty optimistic; we still get turned on, and use the phrase "turned on" unironically. I don't know much about who I am, but I do know where I'm from.

The way this book came about was something like a miracle. The project had been swimming around the shoals of publishing for a long time, lacking focus and energy, crippled by my own doubts. One evening Bill LeBlond, an editor at Chronicle Books, was having dinner with his wife, Adair Lara, the raucous and wise columnist who shares the back page of *The Chronicle* with me on Tuesdays and Thursdays, and Anne Lamott, the gentle, precise, and wonderfully funny novelist who has been a friend of mine since we both worked for Billie Jean King, an experience so weird I have yet to write a column about it.

Oh gosh, they said (so I've been told), isn't it terrible that Jon can't get a book of columns published?

"I think the problem is his selection," said Bill.

"You know," said Adair, "this entire situation makes me despair of the future of humankind."

"And yet, hope springs anew!" exclaimed Annie. "We could read all of Jon's columns and make the selection ourselves!"

And that's what Adair and Annie did. Free for nothing, you understand, out of sheer generosity and friendship, they slogged through literally thousands of columns and picked the best 100. They edited this book, and Annie wrote the introduction, just because it seemed like a good idea.

This stuff doesn't happen in real life; this is fairy-tale material. I think I must have been a very good person in my previous life; something. My debt to them is immense; I literally cannot thank them enough. I do try, of course, but they keep sending the jewelry boxes back unopened.

The book has changed a little since they put the columns together. A few of the ones they chose I rejected for personal reasons; I snuck back in a few favorites that they neglected. No Pele Dancing,* though; they made that a condition of the job.

The columns are not precisely as they appeared in the newspaper; these are not documents. I changed any clunky sentences that leapt out at me; I tacked on new ends when the old ones were impossibly lame. Some two- or three-part columns I edited together as one longer article. Some of the dated jokes I left in; others I changed; it was all a matter of what I could stand to have between slick covers. This book will pass through your life very quickly; it's going to be with me forever.

---

*Don't ask.

I have many people to thank: William German, the executive editor of *The Chronicle*, who gave me the chance to write the column and stuck by me when the arrows started coming; Rosalie Muller Wright (another former employee of Billie Jean King), the Sunday and features editor of *The Chronicle* and an old and valued friend; and Mark Lundgren, my long-suffering and unwholesomely cheerful copy editor.

Thanks too to Richard Geiger and Mike Keiser of *The Chronicle*, and to Bryan Higgins (inventor of the Kramden Utilities, burly companion to the Norton Utilities), who helped maneuver my columns through the shoals of ASCII. I met Bryan through a computer network, a form of communication I recommend to everyone. Comments about this book or anything else reach me fastest by email: jrc@well.sf.ca.us

I owe a great deal to my readers, many of whose names appear here and there throughout the book. All writing is a partnership, but writing a column is particularly so; when I take one of my little walk-abouts, it's nice to know that there are people willing to follow me, willing to work with me and sometimes read it twice. The title of this book was suggested by a reader, Lawrence A. Reh of Alameda, a stranger to me and yet also a collaborator.

History counts too: Great gratitude, for support and good counsel when I needed it most, to William Wong, the late Dick Demorest, John Burks, Jennifer Cressman, Pamela Miller, Julie Smith and B. K. Moran (who is, yes, yet another former employee of Billie Jean King). They know what they did; I hope they know how much I appreciate it.

And thanks and love to my mother, Jane Crane, who taught me to love reading and writing, thereby giving me both a hobby and a career; and to my daughters Rachel and Shana, who taught me that love is real and charity persists and cynicism is always a chump's game.

Moi

TAKING THE JAR FOR A RIDE IN THE CAR.

The instructions for the sperm sample were quite clear: Use a clean dry glass jar, and get it to the hospital within one hour. No problem. I selected a squat cylindrical container, formerly used by seven or nine artichoke hearts, and I left with plenty of time to spare—the hospital is only 10 minutes from my house.

The day was bright, the air was clear, my spirits were uplifted. It occurred to me that I had never taken my sperm for a ride on the freeway before. There they were, snug in my pocket, their little tails waggling furiously, wondering what this unprecedented outing was all about.

I began talking to them; they were my tiny chums; I felt a responsibility. Genetically speaking, they were me, only much smaller and not worried about hair loss.

"There's Lake Merritt," I told them. "Very nice bird sanctuary there; frogs and polliwogs too. You'd like polliwogs; you'd have a lot to talk about, if you talked."

I was warming to my Gray Line tour guide role. "You can just see, or anyway I can just see, a corner of the Bay Bridge. Built during the Depression; in many ways a more impressive engineering feat than the Golden Gate Bridge." These were East Bay sperm; I wanted them to have a sense of history.

We arrived, my sperm and I, at the hospital. We walked into the door marked "Laboratory." There was a line at the desk. "Don't worry," I whispered, only loud enough for the jar to hear, "plenty of time."

Finally, I reached the Person in Charge.

"I have a, I have, you know," I said to the Person.

"No sir, I do not know," she said.

"I have a sample," I said.

"Stool or sperm?"

"Sperm."

She looked at the requisite form in triplicate I was carrying.

"Sir, the label must go on the bottle. Please place the label from the form on the bottle."

"I shall do that," I said, not wanting to do it.

I took the jar out of my pocket and set it on the counter. I sensed that the sperm were embarrassed by this sudden exposure to the larger world. I peeled the label off the form and pressed it on the jar. The label did not stick.

"The label does not stick," I said.

"I'll get you some tape." My sperm and I waited while she got some tape. I examined a corner of the ceiling, pretending that I was merely early to a symphony concert and was killing time. The sperm would have whistled thinly through their lips, had they had lips.

There was suddenly a voice at my elbow. "Hiya, pal, how's it going?" said the voice.

It was Joel Selvin, the popular music critic of this very newspaper. I have known Joel for 15 years and am generally charmed to see him. On this occasion, however, I was less than entirely pleased.

I exchanged a glance with my sperm. I could sense that it wished to remain anonymous.

"Fine, Joel. It goes fine."

He smiled and nodded in his cheerful way.

"So, what brings you down here?" he asked.

A panoply of possibilities crossed my mind. Visiting a sick friend?

Incognito research for a blistering column on hospital procedures? An unhealthy preoccupation with three-year-old issues of *Time* magazine?

"Your tape," said the Person, returned.

I interposed my body between Joel and my sperm. I stuck the label on. Joel looked over my shoulder. I hunched further. I handed the now suitably labeled container to the Person.

"I'll just take this to the incubator," she said.

Joel and I stood there. "So," he said. I agreed instantly.

RECURSIVE AUTO-NOSTALGIA

I was speaking the other day with my friend, the cofounder of NASA, the National Association of Short Adults (their motto: Down In Front!), and we were drifting back to the days when we were all short, although none of us were adults.

Those days I like to think of as childhood.

And I remembered Sight-Savers. I'm not sure they're even sold anymore, but you know what I mean, wallet-sized packets of thin, coated paper used for cleaning glasses.

Sort of a black shiny cover. Sight-Savers.

When I was 9 or 10, on one of those walks home from school that took two hours because there were so many things to investigate, I came across a package of Sight-Savers in the gutter. I had never seen Sight-Savers before, and for some reason (the black cover?) I became convinced that Sight-Savers were linked to the deepest, darkest secrets of the adult world.

You know the secrets to which I refer. The secrets contained in the conversations that are broken off when you enter the room. The girls-are-different-from-boys secrets.

So I took the Sight-Savers home. I didn't tell anyone. I took them home and I put them in the box in my closet where I put things that might one day reveal the inner workings of the world. Weird seed-pods. Coins of foreign origin. Military ribbons. A ring without a stone, eyeless.

I had lots of other stuff in that closet, too, collections mostly. I collected bottle caps, for instance. They were easy to collect; I've never been a particularly hard worker. The guy at the store was happy to get rid of them.

On slow days, I would take all the caps out and line them up by brand. Coke always won; Nehi Orange was always second. Creme Soda (nice light-blue cap) was always last. I felt sorry for Creme Soda and bought a bottle whenever I could. Still, my contribution did not make up for vast public indifference.

I also collected baseball cards, toy soldiers, marbles and stamps. My Catholic friend Mike McCord urged me to collect stamps from the Vatican. I was not exactly sure what the Vatican was, but their stamps were huge and pretty. I also had stamps from San Marino, which was pretty confusing because I lived in Pasadena and San Marino was about a mile away.

Anyway, Sight-Savers. I used to take out my package of Sight-Savers at night and puzzle over their exact function. It didn't occur to me to ask an adult; I had the strong suspicion that the Sight-Savers would be thrown away and never discussed again.

A year went by. The Sight-Savers ceased to dominate my fantasy life, but they didn't lose their magical power. Then one day I was having lunch in the cafeteria when the kid sitting across from me reached into his lunch box and pulled out . . . a packet of Sight-Savers!

Right there! In public! I shrank in horror. What if the girls saw? What if the teachers saw? Permanent vice principal time, for sure. A lifetime in the fifth grade.

Then the kid casually, oh so casually, ripped one sheet of paper out of the Sight-Savers packet and he . . . well, I won't tell you what he did. But it surprised the hell out of me.

SIBLINGHOOD IS POWERFUL

We always think the grass is greener, sometimes because dissatisfaction is the nature of the human condition and sometimes because Mr. Wilson next door is a better gardener.

Tall people dream of being inconspicuous; short people dream of being able to change light bulbs. Beautiful people want to be appreciated for their minds; smart people want to be lusted after mindlessly. People who are both beautiful and smart fret that one quality is being overlooked because of the other.

Me, I came from the smallest possible family: two. Mom and I went through most of my childhood alone together. Naturally, I dreamed fervently of being part of a large family. I occasionally visited large families; I wanted to be more than a visitor.

Here was the thing I liked best about large families: products on the dinner table. Bottles of ketchup and mayonnaise; boxes of cereal and Ritz crackers; cartons of milk. There was something thrilling about all these gaudy commercial items mixed with plates and forks.

The products would be in constant movement, passed from hand to hand, shaken, stirred, their contents occasionally covertly hurled. Mom and I never threw food at each other.

Also, because there was so much on the table, no one actually paid all that much attention to what you ate. In my view, my mother had a fixation on vegetables that bordered on the clinically insane.

In a large family, you could hustle the vegetable question. In my home, the evidence was always in plain sight. Not even a cereal box to hide behind.

There was always noise in large families; great comforting wallows of noise. Many conversations happened simultaneously; each competed with the others for decibel dominance. Sometimes I could just float along on the family sound, bouncing with the rhythm, oblivious to the content.

In my house, my mother spoke and then I spoke, or neither of us spoke. Even our dog was quiet. Everything seemed very distinct and clear; conversation was like a tuning fork in a cathedral. The fuzzy anonymous chaos of a large family was liberating the way Chuck Berry songs on the radio were liberating.

I could say "Big greasy boogers" pretty loud and no one would notice. If I said "Big greasy boogers" at home, my mother would say, "What, dear?" Not an unreasonable question, but not one that I wanted to answer.

But the real center of the appeal of the big family was siblings.

It seemed like a giant club in which you had a lifetime membership, a club of kids banding together against the world.

(I had a club, of course; I even had a clubhouse in my backyard. The trouble was, the kids in my club didn't know they were in it. The first stories I wrote were about my imaginary club. For many years I thought that was some kind of trigger element in my career choice. But many writers come from large families; what's their excuse?)

There were all the trappings of belonging: nicknames, code words, family jokes, teasing rituals. They all seemed enchanting to me. It never occurred to me that they might get oppressive or boring. I thought: If only I could have a nickname.

If only (I thought) I could share a room with another kid. We could fight about it; we could draw a line down the middle of it. We could trash the other kids' rooms. We could giggle until dawn.

And then we would tumble downstairs in the morning, all 11 of us, to a big table set with cereal boxes, and slurp our food and call each other nasty names. Heaven!

THE FIRST TIME

I don't know why the leaders of the Inquisition had to resort to the rack, the Iron Maiden or the burning hot poker in the uncomfortable location. If they'd really wanted to search out heresies and elicit craven confessions, all they'd have to do is set up a little singing recital.

After three minutes of this exquisite torture, the enemies of the church would have been babbling of Satan, admitting to foul practices, betraying their friends and family. "Go back to the pokers," they would have cried pitifully. "Just don't make me sing in public."

I speak as one with firsthand experience. Last weekend, in a rambling house in Piedmont, against my better judgment, I stood at a piano before an audience of assorted lovers of the Voice and favored them with my rendition of "Where'er You Walk" by Handel.

As an emotional experience, it ranks right behind having a gallstone operation, without anesthetic, performed in a blizzard on the top of a 100-foot tower erected at the North Pole.

As the opening notes sounded, I noticed two things: First, my entire head had developed an unaccountable tremor, as though my spinal column had turned into a vigorously plucked violin string; second, I had no idea where my opening note was.

I took a wild stab. I was wrong.

"Stop right there," said my teacher's teacher, an extremely comely woman with a will of steel. "Here's your note," she said, and sang it. I tried to copy the pitch; I failed. Tried again; failed. Then (oh God please give me a heart attack right now) she had everyone in the room sing it. Aha!

I began again. The tremor in my neck moved southward. My kneecaps jiggled up and down in waltz time. My pant legs shook along merrily. A seven-year-old girl in the front row stared at my knees. I glared at her, but she didn't catch my glance—the dance of the knees had riveted her attention.

I stared out at the audience. They were all smiling with great—

albeit somewhat fixed and strained—enthusiasm. I scanned the room several times as my voice did violence to Handel. The grins remained. I had the sudden unshakable perception that cyanide gas had been released in the room and that the face of every person in the audience was set in the final rictus of death, grinning through until the end of the apocalypse, or the song, whichever came first.

The song lasted about 17 years. I had long since forgotten all the careful instructions about breathing, vowel sounds, arching the soft palate and the rest. I was just hanging in there waiting for the house to burn down.

Mercifully, I was finally able to stop singing. There was applause, the same sort of applause that might occur when a particularly painful two-hour kettle drum solo had finally ceased.

Then something remarkable happened. My teacher, who is a tiger at lesson time but one of the great pussycats in other moments, came forward. She had tears running down her cheeks. She put her arm around me.

"I just want to say," she told the audience, "that when this man came to me in January he couldn't even sing 'Happy Birthday.'"

Everyone applauded again. I could see several wiping their eyes. I was completely stunned. I kissed my teacher several times. I made a joke. I got more applause. I walked off, still bewildered by the entire incident.

Another student shook my hand. "I could really feel for you out there," he said. "I could really understand what that was about. That took a lot of courage."

I smiled and said something. There was a strange buzzing in my ears, a strange film on my eyes. I felt, finally, as though I had just appeared in the Special Olympics.

Another triumph for the singing impaired.

MY CHILD. THINK TWICE. THINK TWICE

Odd as it may seem, a few of you out there will one day be called upon to become newspaper columnists. More of you will become convicted felons or, even worse, stockbrokers, but a select few will beat the odds, take VDT in hand and generate opinions the way a sturgeon generates eggs.

Frequently, as I speak to the young people of the Bay Area and ask them for money, I hear the question, "Do you have any advice for aspiring columnists?"

Usually I say, "Lie down in a cool dark place and visualize yourself wearing the garments of an anesthesiologist." Still, some persist, and it is to those wretched few that I address the following cautionary remarks.

Perhaps the most common experience for a person in my profession (and I have spoken to others in the same profession, and all have confirmed the frequency of this interchange) is getting the following comment from a well-meaning stranger:

"Gosh, I really liked something you wrote the other day and I was meaning to tell you about it. I literally laughed out loud. I read it to my roommate. I put it on my refrigerator door. I mailed it to my cousin in Cleveland. And it was about, gosh, now I've forgotten. Isn't that terrible?"

Well, it can't be that terrible because it happens about nine times a week. It's even understandable: People remember the existence of quality long after they've forgotten the details. Three weeks later, you remember that you had a good meal in a restaurant without being able to recite the specifics of the menu.

But here is the advice: Do not embark with your interlocutor on a voyage to discover which column it was that he or she enjoyed so much.

Say merely, "Thank you." If you don't, the subsequent chat will have a way of giving you the willies for many weeks to come. The following dialogue is guaranteed by an independent panel to be almost true and actual in effect if not in actuality.

You: "Well, about when did the column appear?"

Fan: "Oh, in the last two weeks sometime."

You: "Was it maybe one of the garden things?"

Fan: "No, I hate your garden things. I guess you must be really hard up for ideas when you write those, ha ha."

You: "Maybe Magic Balls? A lot of people . . ."

Fan: "Magic Balls? What was that about?"

You: "You sort of had to read it, see, because—"

Fan: "I know what it was. It was when you took that trip with Nachman to Yosemite. Boy, what a wimp that guy is!"

You: "That was Rubenstein. Rubenstein took the trip with Nachman."

Fan: "Oh. Well, if you see Rubenstein, tell him he's got one fan at least. He's a hell of a funny guy."

You: "Sure. I sure will. You bet."

Fan: "And say hi to that Nachman. I was just kidding about his being a wimp and all. Nobody for President; I still remember that."

One more thing: Occasionally you will arrive at the very end of a column and still have just a little room left over. For those occasions, it is useful to have a small collection of quips and one-liners, something amusing and snappy with a tight, cogent punchline with some really good writing contained in it too.

MY BRILLIANT RADIO CAREER

It was not personal. It is important that we not lose sight of that: It was not personal. The chemistry; it may have been the chemistry. It may have been a failure of communication. It may have been that I was bad.

No, not bad. The word bad was never used. The budget was mentioned; the recession; the direction of management thinking vis-à-vis my thinking. These thinkings diverged at a point in time not readily apparent to the outside observer but entirely clear in retrospect.

So I was fired. Not fired personally, you understand; the idea of me was fired. It's just that we happen to share the same checking account.

They say that failure is the last great taboo in American society. But for someone in my business, failure is something more poignant.

Failure is Thursday's column.

I had a radio show. Sort of. I had a place on the radio where I spoke wisely and wittily with Peter B. Collins, who filled in the blank spots where my wit and wisdom failed. Ten minutes every Thursday.

The audience response was overwhelming. Just like that, I went on the St. Helena Chamber of Commerce mailing list. In all my years at *The Chronicle,* that's never happened. Total strangers stopped me on the street and asked me the way to Chinatown. How they knew I was a radio personality I'll never know.

The response from my friends was very gratifying, ranging as it did from "what time are you on again?" to "tell me once more what time you're on." My wife kept forgetting to listen. It was like living here and having a radio show in Juneau.

In the six months I was there, the radio station deconstructed itself. The first time I walked in, it was bustling with salesmen and junior executives and smart young women in business suits.

Gradually, the place got emptier. They were moving to new, "downsized" offices. One week many of the rooms were filled with boxes. The next week the receptionist was gone. The next week the hall was dark and the door was locked.

There was a sign on the door. It said: "Astrid Gilberto: Ring Bell."

With only the on-air folks left, it was kind of like a college radio station. People ate Top Ramen and threw wads of paper at each other. They discussed the idiosyncrasies of top management. It was very relaxed; I was very relaxed. Maybe too relaxed. Is America ready for on-air napping?

I never did get the hang of the buttons. I kept pressing "Talk Back" when I should have been pressing "On." Several times my voice appeared in the middle of commercial announcements. I felt free to chat with the traffic reporters, which was not always fine with the traffic reporters.

I pressed the "Cough" button several times after I coughed. There are chimpanzees in labs all over America who understand buttons better than I do.

I was not, in actual truth, very good. Often my brain would take a hike in the desert, leaving my mouth behind like a motorized vehicle, its engine still running. On the other hand, this is the station that carries Rush Limbaugh, America's hatemonger to the yahoos. What does "good" mean in that context?

There's a lot wrong with the radio business. My firing is not one of them, but maybe I can pretend it is. In two years, my story will be that I quit after they tried to censor me.

I know that my literally tens of radio fans will back me up.

I THINK I'M LOSING MY WHATCHAMACALLIT

I first realized that I was losing vital brain functions when. . . well, I can't remember the first time I realized it. I think it was right around that big holiday in September, the picnic one. You know.

It was right around that picnic holiday that we were with Fred and Fred's wife Una. Not Una. Edith? Can that be right? Starts with a vowel, though. Irene? Doesn't matter. We were eating dinner at that place right behind the place where the symphony plays.

I remember it clearly because it was the first time I had that fish with the funny name. Orange something. The fish itself was not actually orange; I remember noticing that. Orange roughneck. That can't be right. Came on a plate.

Well, of course it came on a plate. Ha ha. So we were with Fred and Utne at that doodah restaurant, two syllables, and Fred said to me, "In your new glasses, you look just like. . . ." Now I can't remember.

Fred remembered the name of the Russian guy. You know the one: Finland Station, buried in a tomb. Not Stalin. Come on, everyone knows him; he's really really famous. Wore glasses that looked a lot like my glasses. People used to say he looked a lot like Frank Bardacke. That Russian guy.

Frank Bardacke. Isn't he famous? Who am I thinking of? William Hurt? Is William Hurt the Elephant Man guy, or is that John Hurt? Or John Heard? Which one wears the glasses?

Doesn't matter. Fred says to me, *roughy*. That's the name of the fish. Fred doesn't say that; I just remembered it. Whew. Orange roughy. Remembered it right off. Boy, for a minute there I thought I'd really lost it, ha ha.

So this was a really interesting moment, when Fred says to me that in my new glasses I look just like you know. Because when he said that, I said: "What glasses?"

I had forgotten that I was wearing glasses! And that was weird because I'd gotten my glasses only the week before at the Whatsie Center, you know, the one with the phone number that ends in 2020, very cute.

Maybe you don't know. But I should remember because I was really irritated that I had to get prescription reading glasses instead of those $10 jobbies I get at the place near the freeway with the big parking lot. But I have to get the expensive kind because I have asymmetricism.

Not asymetricism. That's not even a word. That thing that people get that's neither farsighted nor nearsighted. It's the other thing. I have it. And the net result is that I have two pair of glasses except usually I don't because I can't remember where I put them.

I've learned to look in the refrigerator. You get crafty after a while. No matter what I've lost, I look for it in the refrigerator. And I can always find the refrigerator.

It's right next to the small box that cooks things with waves.

Where was I? Refrigerator, glasses, fish, that Russian guy, Elephant Man. . . wait a minute. Were we talking about the Elephant Man? Why would we do that? Wonderful movie, though. David Lynch, Mel Brooks, Marla Ekberg.

But. . . no, wait. Marla Ekberg was my girlfriend in the ninth grade. What a stupid mistake. It was that other actress. . . Anne Bancroft. That's it! Married to Mel Brooks, who produced *The Elephant Man* directed by David Lynch and starring John Hurt!

That should dispel any rumors about my memory. I've welcomed this opportunity to demonstrate my continued competence. Have you seen my shoes?

GETTING A HOLE IN THE LOBE

Is it too late for an earring? I suppose it is. Earrings on males have been around for a few years now; probably time for them to go back out of style. Maybe they're already out of style; maybe I just haven't gotten my bulletin in the mail.

I was thinking of getting one, but I'm not sure. Maybe I could experiment with clip-ons, but I don't think clip-ons are happening for guys. One palmate shell grasping each lobe, hanging on for dear life—not a guy thing. It's the hole or nothing; earwear macho.

Do I want to sit in a department store while a jewelry clerk wounds me in the nicest possible way? Am I ready for posts? I don't think so, but I'm not sure.

It was like this with ponytails. First guys with hair started wearing ponytails, and I didn't pay attention. Then baldish guys like me started wearing ponytails, and I thought they looked silly. Then guys balder than me, real cue-ball-and-fringe fellas, started wearing ponytails, and I started seriously considering the matter.

But then earrings intruded; earrings dominated the landscape. A diamond stud, maybe. I don't think I'm ready for a dangling cross, but I'm not sure. Nothing really huge and jangling: I don't want to look like a Berkeley poetess. I don't think I can handle a serape.

Maybe dolphins. Maybe I could wear dolphins ironically. But I don't think so.

My beard is 20 years old. I just realized that, and I wish I hadn't. My beard is old enough to vote or drive a car. I haven't seen my chin since 1969.

I have a daughter younger than my beard.

Of course, it's not the same beard. Hair is replaced completely every seven years, so I've had almost three different beards. But it's really the same beard, a beard that should settle down and start thinking about the future.

My beard has seen a lot. My beard has seen the rise and fall and rise again of beards. My beard has seen Watergate, the Star Trek movies, Shirley MacLaine's astral projections, the Nintendo Cereal System, Bhopal. My beard has been frozen in Chicago and baked in Bikaner.

We have to consider a young lobe hole and an old beard. Are they compatible, in terms of personal style? Be candid. No, don't be candid. I can work this out for myself.

Today is my birthday. It cannot be coincidental that I would be thinking about testosterone-linked earrings on my birthday. I understand that; I am alive to undercurrents.

I don't mind that it's my birthday. Getting old really does have advantages. Not pretend-to-keep-your-spirits-up advantages, but actual pluses. I can use most household appliances without fear now. The only downside is that I'm closer to death.

Death is not an upbeat kind of deal.

And people with earrings don't die. Think about the movies you've seen. "He died with his earrings on"—people don't say that. Winston Churchill: No earrings, now dead. Helen Gurley Brown: Wears earrings, still alive. It may be coincidence, but why take a chance?

On the other hand, it might look ridiculous. Would you want to live forever if everyone thought you'd looked ridiculous? Eternity is an awful long time to be a jerk. Let me think about it. We'll talk more.

THE CALPURNIA OF COMB-OVERS

The first thing to realize, the first and most important thing to realize, is that I do not have a comb-over. I have never had a comb-over. Any imputations that I have now or have ever had a comb-over are utterly without foundation.

I hold in my hand affidavits—long, lustrous, naturally curly affidavits. You may read them at your leisure.

The true comb-over, the kind I do not have, involves letting the hair on the side of the head just above the ear grow unnaturally long. These lengthy tresses are then taken by oxen across the broad barren prairie of the top scalp and secured above the other ear.

The precise function of the comb-over is fraught with deep psychological mystery. Ostensibly, the comb-over is designed to simulate a full head of hair, a sort of makeshift toupee.

But a comb-over never looks anything like a full head of hair. A comb-over looks only like a comb-over. Scientists are still not clear about the level of self-deception involved. Do men with comb-overs look in the mirror and say: "My, what a darned fine mane of hair I have now?" Or do they say: "This should be pathetic enough for even the most demanding sadist?"

It's a matter of messages. The apparent message of the comb-over is, "Here is a man who has not lost his youthful vigor." The actual message of the comb-over is, "Here is a man desperately worried about losing his youthful vigor."

By youthful vigor, you understand, I mean . . . you know, vigor. It's very psychological, and not the sort of thing you'd talk about at the check-out counter.

For a male with somewhat less hair than previously, the comb-over pitfall is complicated by the topknot. Male pattern baldness very frequently leaves an island of hair at the crest of the forehead.

One goes about one's life. Let me be clear about this: I go about my life. I part my hair on the right; I comb the hair to the left. Looks like

22

anyone else's hair. Gradually, twin inroads are made due north from the outside tip of each eyebrow. Scalp inexorably appears.

And then something dreadful happens. In combing the topknot over the fjord of scalp, I notice that the net effect very much resembles a comb-over. It is not a comb-over, of course, because a comb-over involves growing the hair just above the ear long. I am clear on this.

But it looks like a comb-over. This is unacceptable. In the matter of comb-overs, I am Calpurnia.

Calpurnia, grateful scholars will recall, was Caesar's wife. Caesar's wife was required not just to refrain from extramarital dalliances, but also to refrain from giving the appearance of indulging in extramarital dalliances. Her image had to be as pristine as her reality.

So it is with me and comb-overs. It is not enough to be peaceful in my own mind; I have to make sure that the world understands that I am peaceful in my own mind. I suspect this may have to do with the vigor thing, but I am not a licensed psychologist.

So now I have this haircut. That is the bottom line. My haircut is such that I no longer require a comb. Without a comb, there can be no comb-over. Scientists agree on this point. My head is now skull-shaped; no softening waves of hair.

I look in the mirror and see a bullet-headed retired Army officer.

This is unnerving, but at least it's vigorous. Perhaps I will purchase a uniform and a large pistol. If anyone mentions comb-overs, I will just shoot him with my big gun.

WHEN A GUY HUGS A GUY

When I was growing up, guys didn't hug guys. I take that back. Guys probably did hug guys, but they certainly didn't do it in public and they certainly didn't tell me about it.

Guys shook the hands of other guys. That was what guys did.

Later on, I became aware that guys hugged guys, but the guys who hugged guys were guys who thought of guys in a romantic manner. Still later, it was widely put about that all guys should hug all other guys (not absolutely strange guys, but good friends and maybe even firm acquaintances, depending on the profession of the guy in question—it's OK to hug a painter guy, not so OK to hug a stockbroker guy), and so I went about hugging guys when I believed that it was socially proper to do so.

(Ever notice how a word loses its meaning when you type it, or say it, often enough? In the last 20 minutes, the word "guy" has lost all denotation; I'm working entirely on semantic memory here.)

Now, guys were not particularly good at guy-hugging, what with lack of practice and all, so the first few years of sanctioned heterosexual guy-hugging were a little rocky.

The baseline hug posture—arms around each other's trunks—went well enough, but questions continually popped up about other portions of the body.

Some guys elected to bend from the waist, like British gentlemen smelling peonies, so that nothing but shoulders and cheeks came into contact.

The embrace of two guys with that hugging philosophy, embracing, resembled the start of a Greco-Roman wrestling match.

Other guys went for the bear hug approach, an embrace so intensely masculine and physical that both participants experienced actual pain. This transcended the question of physical contact by turning the embrace into a contest of wills.

When a person of the latter school met a person of the former school, one or the other was likely to tip over and slide to the floor. As a way of expressing New Age affection, it left something to be desired.

There were other, subtler difficulties. I, for instance, have a hug buddy (I'm not sure why I hug some of my male friends but not others, but I do know that once you've entered into a hug-on-meeting relationship, there's no turning back; I would take it as a sign of incipient loathing if one of my usual huggees offered his hand to me instead) who is perhaps six inches taller than I.

I am not used to hugging very tall people. I have to stand on tiptoe to make sure my chin surmounts his shoulder in the approved manner. Since he is also a bear hugger, I have had occasionally to stand on my toes until my calves cramped up.

Then I've had to stifle my boyish cries of agony while muttering "How's it goin', guy" through clenched teeth.

This tall friend has for some time worn a small gold earring. Nothing fancy; just a little hemisphere the size of an ant shish-kabobing his left lobe.

Lately, however, he has taken to wearing a more dangling ornament. Every time we hug, this appendage rakes my cheek or pokes me in the eye. In an effort to avoid instant blindness, I have had to bury my face in his shoulder, leading onlookers to believe that I have been overcome by grief.

We've come a long way, baby, but we ain't there yet. Maybe we should go back to shaking hands until some international safety standards are formulated.

ON THE NOTION OF HAVING A CHAIR

My father had a chair. It was a big rattan number with a gaudy tropical print and a matching footstool. It was strategically placed close to the window with a panoramic view of the Pacific Ocean.

On the table next to my father's chair was a huge, two-handled coffee cup, "For Two-Fisted Drinkers." Also a bean-bag ashtray and a carton of Camels. On the bookshelf behind the chair was a radio permanently tuned to the station that carried the Dodger games. He had only to reach behind him to turn it on; he didn't have to look.

Sometimes he did that in the middle of a party, just to get a quick hit of the current score. My father once had a dog that responded to the name Julian Javier by rolling on the floor and barking. Javier, during those years, was a good-field, no-hit infielder for the St. Louis Cardinals. Neither my father nor his dog nor I ever tired of that trick.

There was something implicitly nautical about his chair, an aura reinforced by the general oceanic decor of his house. It was the captain's chair, the seat of power. The great domestic ship was controlled from that chair.

"All ahead full," he would seem to say, and there were anecdotes and laughter.

My stepfather (who is unlike my father in almost every way) had two chairs, the living room chair and the dining room chair. Both chairs were large, although my stepfather was not a particularly bulky man.

When my stepfather sat in his chair (either chair), it was as though a rolling current of calm had passed through his body. He was livelier and more garrulous in either of his chairs than he was in other regions of the house.

There were rules for his chairs, even as there were rules for my father's chair. They were the same rules. It was OK to sit in the chair when the incumbent was not in the home; it was not OK to sit in the chair at any other time, even when the chair was not in use.

I knew the rules; as far as I remember, I did not resent them. Someday, I may have thought to myself, I will have my own chair. It will invest me with its power.

I will be the head of the household. I will have a chair.

And so I did; two chairs. We may, for purposes of this column, gloss over a feminist analysis along the lines of "The Furniture of Oppression: A Critique of the Male Chair." I cede the point. I am willing to cede all sorts of points; I just want to retain my chairs.

Surprisingly, the other members of my family (three members, all female) were mostly willing to postulate my implicit control of my chairs.

Once, my older daughter sat in my chair. I came into the room and stood over her.

"Ahem," I said.

"Yes?" she said, with unconvincing innocence.

"My . . . chair," I said. "This is my chair."

"Why is it your chair?" she asked.

"I am unable," I said, "to describe in rational terms precisely why this chair is my chair. Nevertheless, this chair is indeed my chair."

"That seems fair," she said, unexpectedly. She got up. I sat down. A feeling of unshakable peace suffused my body.

"Fair? Really? How so?" I asked.

She shrugged. "You're very old."

That seemed fair.

THE ODD INCIDENT AT MACY'S

Much later, there were some questions concerning motivation. People who know the full story, however, have no such questions. I will tell you the full story; you may judge for yourself.

First: I have long been looking for pants with an elastic waistband and front pockets. Pants like that fit the way I live today; even better, pants like that fit the shape I am today. Mostly, in the world of adult pants, there is the belt-assisted garment. That was precisely what I did not want.

Second: I am not an enthusiastic shopper. I will shop when I must, because I have needs, but I do not enjoy it. Other people say, "Let's go shopping," using the same tone of voice in which they would say, "Let's go to the movies!"

When I say, "Let's go shopping," I use the same tone of voice in which I would say, "Let's get a bone marrow transplant!" My one principle of shopping is this: Let's see if they have it at Macy's. I like Macy's because I know where it is; that's important in a store. Also I think there's a little *Miracle on 34th Street* working in my relationship with Macy's. Maybe Glinda the Good will wait on me at Macy's; I hold out that hope.

If the item in question isn't at Macy's, perhaps it's time for a nice nap. That is my philosophy of shopping.

So we have the desire for the pants with the elastic waistband and the front pockets, and we have the trip to Macy's. I question the clerk in the pants department about the matter; she tells me to go downstairs.

Downstairs is a little looser, a little funkier, a little kicked-back chill-out faux-Cuban Macy's. A good Macy's, but a different Macy's. Within seconds, I find the pants I am looking for.

I take them into the changing room. (I really hate the changing room, with those weird doors like an Old West saloon. Are they ankle fetishists at Macy's? Do they think I'm going to stuff a pair of pants in my shoes?)

The pants fit splendidly, like a dream, better than I could have imagined. Using advice gleaned long ago from a Shopping Fool friend of mine ("If you find something you like, buy more than one"), I buy three pairs of these wonderful pants.

The other thing the Shopping Fool told me was never to try to save money on shoes. She said—but I seem to be delaying the moment of revelation, the catch (as it were) in this cheerful story of retail satisfaction. Very well:

The pants are called Surf Boyz. Surf Boyz have elastic at the cuffs as well as at the waist; Surf Boyz tend to bag around the calves like pantaloons.

You've seen Surf Boyz. Lot of 15-year-olds wear 'em. Some designs even feature the Surf Boy himself, an odd, angular figure, crudely drawn in a kind of neo-cave painting style. The Surf Boy has a flattop haircut and splayed toes; he is carrying a spear.

The Surf Boy is gray. His spear is fluorescent orange. He is all over my legs even as I type these words.

The reaction to the Surf Boyz has been mixed. Both of my daughters, so very different in so many ways, said exactly the same thing. "You have new pants," they each said, using a particularly flat, neutral, I-can-jump-either-way-on-this-one tone of voice. Having a zany dad can be a real strain.

"Like 'em?" I asked, that fatherly twinkle high in my eye.

One said: "You look like half the guys in my school."

The other said: "Like is a really hard concept for me right now."

CONFESSIONS OF A TAX CHEAT

Thank heavens the IRS is finally cracking down on free-lance writers. For too long have these parasites been allowed to live high on the hog (or at least halfway up the hog) at the expense of honest wage earners.

Free-lance writers get to spend entire days in their bathrobes while others are dressing for success. They get to stay home while less fortunate citizens must brave the daily commute.

If you've ever seen a free-lance writer at work, you already know that most of his or her time is spent staring at cracks in the ceiling and trying to form animal faces out of them.

"If you squint, you can see a bear," a free-lance writer will tell the first person who comes along. This is a day's work for a free-lance writer.

And free-lance writers get to work for some of the noblest people in this nation: magazine editors. In 1935, a feature article in a national magazine would be worth (to the writer of said article) about $5000.

Today, 52 years later, a feature article in a national magazine is still worth about $5000.

Magazine editors have controlled the inflationary spiral. Politicians in Washington may spend money like water, but not magazine editors. They've been willing to make the hard choices.

Not that the free-lance writers were any help. All they did was whine.

Justice, however, has finally prevailed. The new tax code specifically and harshly limits the amount of deductions free-lance writers can take. It says, in essence, that a project must make money before deductions can be taken for expenses.

That right there eliminates 98 percent of the free-lance writers in this country. The point of free-lance writing is not to make money. The point of free-lance writing is to wear a bathrobe in the afternoon.

I have myself been a free-lance writer, and I know the kind of blatant cheating that goes on. I shudder to confess that I have done it myself.

For instance, stamps. I deducted the cost of stamps, because I had to mail my query letters and manuscripts and revisions and second revisions and letters inquiring about payment and further letters inquiring about payment and angry letters demanding payment; all the cost of doing business.

But some of the stamps I used for personal correspondence or bills or sweepstakes entries. Some of the stamps I just plain lost. And yet I deducted them.

Of course, since I only made $11,000 that year, the loss to the taxpayers was not significant. But it's the principle of the thing. And the interest, of course, except we're way beyond the statute of limitations.

And typing paper. I used some of that typing paper to mop up spilled glasses of pear nectar. Pear nectar takes a lot of paper, every single sheet fully deducted.

Multiply my bogus deductions by the number of free-lance writers in the nation (seems like about 100 million), and the cost to the American treasury is incalculable, at least by a free-lance writer.

Now that the IRS has finally nailed free-lance writers, I hope it will turn its attention to the really big fish in the tax-avoidance pond: the conceptual artists. You know, the my-life-is-my-art crowd. Forget Ivan Boesky; go after the folks who charge $5 to watch them kiss Chevrolets.

FATHER OF DAUGHTERS PLAYS WITH BOYS

I never had a son; I never regretted it for a moment. My years spent being vaguely helpful at nursery schools only reinforced my feeling; little boys are the less amiable of the two available sexes.

Why would I want a son? As soon as he reached adolescence, he'd want to kill me and marry my wife.

And yet . . . I was at a house party in Stinson Beach with a lot of people I didn't know. Some of the people were young boys. It was a dank, glowering day; wind out of the northwest at 15 knots; the second day of summer here in the fog belt of Pacific Rim.

I walked on the beach, anyway; I'll take gloomy weather over disjointed conversation any day.

I walked as long as I could without seeming clinically antisocial. When I returned to the dunes one of the boys yelled at me.

"Bad guy coming," he said. "Get the gun from the fort!"

I began making bad guy noises, which sounded a lot like a ballpark organ encouraging the home team to hit a home run. "DUM dum dum dum, DUM dum dum dum, DUM dum dum dum," I said, walking stiff-legged in the sand.

The boy ran down the dune. "Are you a bad guy?"

"Definitely. DUM dum dum dum, DUM dum dum dum."

He kicked furiously at the sand. He was 10 feet away and three feet tall; I was in no immediate danger. I spun, staggered and dropped to the sand.

"How about if I be a good guy?" I asked. Falling down in the sand is not as much fun as it used to be.

"You want to be in our fort?" he asked. Another boy appeared over the edge of the dunes. He pointed his stick at me. "Bang," he said.

"Tell your friend I'm a good guy," I said to the kid nearest me. He waved frantically. "Stop shooting NOW!" he said.

"Bang bang," said the boy with the stick. What we had here was a failure to communicate.

Jack was the boy who had challenged me initially; Matthew was the lad with the stick. Jack, who was perhaps 7 to Matthew's perhaps 5, did most of the talking.

"You can join our fort," he said. "Sign these papers."

He handed me some imaginary papers; I signed them with a flourish. He took them back and handed me something else. "Autograph," he said.

Autograph? I signed it and handed it back. That was the wrong thing to do. He looked at me impatiently. "Autograph *card*," he said. So very different. I pocketed the card and thanked him. "I'm the captain," he reminded me.

"What can I be?" asked Matthew. "How about if you be the boss?" I said, using a hard-won trick of corporate life.

Having established dominance and hierarchy, we decided to take a walk on the beach. "Let's go to the bad-guy airplane," said Jack, meaning the kite being flown by the edge of the water.

Our progress was slowed by Matthew, who liked to die a lot. He'd spin and fall about every 90 seconds. Jack or I would administer CPR.

Jack found a dead crab. Matthew got tired of dying and played "don't let the ocean catch you" on the shiny sands by the water. Jack and I didn't want to play; one of us was worried about getting his shoes wet. "Can I hold your hand?" Jack asked.

"Yes," I said.

"I'm good at science," said Jack.

"Ah," I said. "Does your father teach you science?"

"Mr. Wizard," said Jack. We walked on. I figured, if I'd had a son, he'd give Mr. Wizard all the credit too.

UNFISHING IN AMERICA: THE INNER VOYAGE

We were an island in a river of women. Susan Faludi, author of *Backlash*, had just finished talking about the attempted destruction of the feminist movement by fearful and selfish men, and Tim and I had sought each other out.

Not that we had been bothered by being one third of the total number of males in attendance. Not at all. Perhaps we had felt some shame for our gender-mates, but it was the good shame, the enlightening shame. We felt that way even though, as men, we had pretty much gotten our own way for 5000 years.

Tim and I hate getting our own way.

"I have an idea for a column," said Tim.

"We're bonding," I said.

"We are beyond bonding," said Tim.

"Absolutely. I keep forgetting. Bonding is all that discredited Robert Bly garbage. We're just friends. We don't feel the need to compete; we are unthreatened by strength in others. And yet, we don't make a big deal of it. We don't yammer on and on about the nature of our relationship. We don't—"

"The New Fishing," said Tim. The river of women flowed on.

"I am unaware of the new fishing," I said. The noise level in the room was intense; our noses were four inches apart.

"I went fishing with Dick," he said. He pointed to Dick, who was one-sixth of the males in the room. "Dick can tell you more about it than I can."

Dick was upcurrent. "Why don't you tell me about it?" I said.

"Remember how it was when we were kids? We'd go fishing and we'd catch a fish and get it up on the dock and watch it flop around and then we'd gut it and clean it and eat it, unless it wasn't any good. But we'd kill it. That was the point."

Tim and I had very different childhoods. In my childhood, we did not kill fish. There are no trout streams in Pasadena. Once in a while some underprivileged kids—I qualified; my family was rich in culture but poor in, you know, money—were loaded on a bus and taken down to San Pedro and herded onto a boat and propelled out into the Catalina Channel where we sat ashen-faced smelling the live bait until it was time to come home.

"Sure, I remember that," I said. That would seem on the surface to be a lie, but it was really more of a conversational convenience. If we ever really got into it, I'd cheerfully admit that I was not a youthful sportsman.

In fact, I'm admitting it now. Tim will read this; the next time we meet we'll clasp each other about the shoulders and laugh with unforced amusement.

"They don't kill the fish anymore," said Tim. "They just kind of catch one and look at it."

"Look at it?"

"They're pretty, fish. Dick has this really light line that any fish could break in a minute. If the fish is so stupid that it doesn't break the line, Dick just reels it in and holds it underwater and looks at it. Then he lets it go."

"That seems very humane," I said. I was trying to encourage Tim to articulate his feelings.

"Oh yeah oh yeah, it's humane enough. Definitely humane." Tim seemed dubious.

"It would be even more humane if you stayed home entirely."

"Well, that's sort of it," said Tim. "From my point of view. Although I had a really good time, and the fish were pretty. But it was a different kind of a deal."

The river of women flowed on.

A SONG OF THANKS; A GRAT ETUDE

Thanksgiving has always been my favorite holiday. It's comfortably free of the strident religious and/or militaristic implications that give other holidays their soft, uneasy undertones. At Christmas, for example, we are required to deal with the divinity of Christ—I know some of you folks out there have made up your mind about that one, but not me—and on the Fourth of July we must wrestle with the question of whether all those simulated aerial bombardments are the most useful form of nationalism available.

At Thanksgiving, all we have to worry about is whether we can wholeheartedly support (a) roasted turkey, (b) friends and (c) gratitude. My opinion on these matters is unambiguous; I am in favor of all of them. The thrill of Thanksgiving is thus undiminished by caveats, codicils or carps. That alone is something to be thankful for.

Thanksgiving provides a formal context in which to consider the many instances of kindness and charity that have enlightened our lives. Kindness and charity are fine and sentimental subjects for contemplation.

First, there are the public personalities, artists and entertainers and philosophers, who have been there when they were needed, whether they knew it or not. Let us think pleasant thoughts about Otis Spann and Duke Ellington; Salman Rushdie and Anthony Burgess; Sigrid Wurschmidt and Mary Mason; Roberto Clemente and Will Clark; Stephanie Salter and Deborah Amos; Seamus Heany and Wallace Stevens; Bonnie Simmons and Etta James—this is my partial list; feel free to create your own.

And there are the teachers, the men and woman who took the time to fire a passion for the abstract, for the continuity of history and the adventure of the future. Our society seems bent on underpaying and ignoring its teachers—at its peril, and at ours.

Even closer. Companions. We all learned about sex from somebody, and that person deserves a moment of remembrance. Somebody taught us a hard lesson about life, told us something unpleasant for our own good, and that willingness to risk conflict for friendship is worth a pause this day. And somebody sat with us through one long night, and listened to our crazy talk and turned it toward sanity; that person has earned this moment too.

And a moment for old friends now estranged, victims of the flux of alliances and changing perceptions. There was something there once, and that something is worth honoring.

Our parents, of course, and our children; our grandparents and our grandchildren. We are locked in the dance of life with them and, however tedious that dance can sometimes seem, it is the rhythm of our lives; to ignore it is to deny our heritage and our legacy.

And thanks, too, for all the past Thanksgivings, and for all the people we shared them with. Thanks for the time the turkey fell on the floor; for the time that Uncle Benny was persuaded to sing "Peg O' My Heart;" for the time two strangers fell in love, and two lovers fell asleep in front of the fire, even before the pumpkin pie.

And the final bead on the string is for this very Thanksgiving, this particular Thursday, and for the people we will be sharing it with. Whoever they are and whatever the circumstances that have brought us together, we will today be celebrating with them the gift of life and the persistence of charity, in a world that seems bent on destroying one and denying the other.

Thanks. A lot.

ETERNAL LIFE: BANE OR BOON?

So now there is a human growth hormone that can give me the body of a 20-year-old. I believe this to be an evolutionarily unsound idea, although it would be of great personal value. I could cut a wide swath through the gene pool if my experience and charm were packaged for the youth market.

Fabulous fantasy. I spent 20 minutes with it last night; just wonderful. Everything I've learned in 46 years put into a low-mileage chassis—honey, the women of America would not stand a chance.

It's a high concept, but it's a crummy idea. It's a nice Tom Hanks movie or something, but it's cosmically tacky. It's taking science in the wrong direction; it's switching carts and horses. It's denying the inevitability of the inevitable; it's the ultimate tautology.

It's true that we don't need more people just now. We certainly don't need more vigorous, ambitious people competing for space and power and, having gotten same, wanting to make more babies. But that's not what I'm talking about.

I'm talking about how the world needs old people as much as it needs young people. I'm saying that there's nothing the matter with age, although there's a lot wrong with a society that thinks of aging as a villain to be conquered. I'm talking about the up side of death. This is the only column you will read today on that subject.

It's like those fires in Southern California. Terrible, yes, blah blah; terrible every time they happen, which is every year. It should be every year. It's a coastal desert down there; the chaparral ecology that has developed depends on the inevitable fires to thrive.

The fire cleans out all the dead stuff; the fire pops the seed pods and propagates the seeds. The nutrients in the ash feed new growth. And then it starts happening again. Taking the long view, the fire is just setting the stage for the next fire.

Because we insist on building flammable structures in a fire zone, the structures burn down periodically. It's not necessary for the life cycle of humans to endure a fire, but we're a smallish bit of the puzzle. Our needs are not primary.

The hillsides need to die in order to live. Everywhere nature is eating its own, feeding on itself. Earth is a closed system; it has nowhere else to get its nutrients.

So we come to the notion of a reductionist society whose only measure of life is its length. The only recognized currency is time; the only acknowledged enemy is death. That is not a lesson of nature; that is something we made up ourselves.

If I were to suddenly have 20 years tacked on to my life span—and not the next 20 years; the last 20 years relived—what the hell would I do with it? The first two weeks, sure, but after that? Get confused and sullen, is my guess.

I've been sort of humming along on my biological clock, figuring three score years and ten or so, setting myself up within that context.

There are immense satisfactions—and fears and losses and pain. It has a particular texture, different from 10 years ago, different from 20 years ago. And I know that the fire will come; that won't change. And if the fire has to come, I want to have cherished every part of my life equally. How could I be a father to my adult children if I'm a surly octogenarian in the body of a lifeguard? How could I understand the story of my life if I'm forever rereading chapter three?

Eternal youth is not a virtue; fear of death is not a philosophy.

THE LAST FRIDAY OF EVERY MONTH

On the last Friday of every month, the Protestant chaplain at San Francisco General Hospital conducts a memorial service for the people who have died at the hospital that month.

On that Friday, at around 12:30, chaplain Tim Greene leaves his office on the second floor of the main building and walks about 30 steps to the back door of the small chapel. Usually, a few of the celebrants of the noon Mass are still there, tidying up. They leave quickly.

He looks out over the small room, seven rows of polished wooden pews. There is rarely anyone there whom he doesn't recognize; there is rarely anyone there except the full-time secretary at the chaplaincy office and whichever dutiful Episcopal volunteer is on duty.

Occasionally, the Catholic priest attached to the hospital will attend as a demonstration of ecumenical solidarity. But mostly it's three people in a quiet room with an altar, three people gathered to remember the unremembered. Some of the people who die at S.F. General leave grieving families; too many do not.

When my friend Annie and I showed up at the service recently, it was described as an occasion. Our presence almost doubled the number of people in the room. Annie's plain alto and my uncertain baritone added unfamiliar color to "The King of Love my Shepherd Is."

The announced hymn had been "Oh God Our Help in Ages Past," but it was thought that "The King of Love my Shepherd Is" might be a little easier on the newcomers. Anything to encourage attendance, I suppose; if they had to go all the way back to "Jesus Loves Me," I imagine they would do it.

The hymn was the final event in the order of service; before the hymn came the reading of the names. We gathered around the altar; it seemed to de-emphasize the emptiness of the room. Tim Greene handed a book to Annie. The names of all the dead had been transcribed lovingly into the book. She read a name; we said, "Rest in peace."

Juan, rest in peace. Peaches, rest in peace. Richard, rest in peace. Foo, rest in peace. A line from Sweeney Todd occurred to me: "They went to their Maker impeccably shaved." Juan and Peaches and Richard and Foo went to their maker with a formal introduction.

I kept imagining the scene without me in it, the scene as it happens most months. That was what struck me as most moving. Tim Greene and the two people he works with, standing in the chapel (cold on that winter day; quiet enough to hear the squeak of gurneys hurrying by), passing a book between them, reciting names.

They are not required by regulation or policy to be there. Their work is among the sick and the dying, and that is mostly what they do. They're obviously not doing it for show—hardly anyone knows they're there.

They're doing it because it seemed important to say that each life is worth dignity, that each death deserves notice. I could say that this message is particularly important just now, with a war raging in Kuwait, but that's not true: It is just as important when there is no prime-time slaughter.

At San Francisco General, there is always a battle. There are always casualties.

We finished reading the names; we rested our last peace. Tim Greene let the silence hang there. Silence extended becomes a receptacle; we each thought what we felt like thinking about mortality.

Death moves beyond profound quickly. Death is sensual, even in church. Especially in church.

Then we began to sing the hymn, not well but not too badly, and then we finished singing the hymn. There was a small change in the room. It was as though a cup, balanced precariously on a windowsill, had been carried over to the center of the table.

My Immediate Surroundings

THE CASE OF THE MISSING CARPENTER

Next door to my home in Oakland is a building that serves, more or less, as a halfway house for Afghan refugees. A family moves in, fresh from two years or so in a camp in Pakistan. The children enroll in school; the young adults look for jobs; the older folks stay home.

Then, at about the time at least some of them have learned English and we can begin to communicate, the family moves out and is replaced by another, cousins or nieces or even more distant relations. They are always exemplary neighbors—hospitable, friendly, considerate—but the language barrier does inhibit in-depth interactions.

A few days ago, late in the afternoon, one of the daughters from the current family appeared at my front door.

"Carpenter," she said. "Gone."

"Your carpenter is gone?" I asked.

"In back. Watching TV." Her eyes looked worried.

"Your carpenter is in back watching TV?" I clearly wasn't getting the drift.

She looked exasperated. "Come," she said. We went out onto the front lawn. The entire family was standing outside. Their faces were drawn; their brows were knitted.

"Carpenter gone," said the girl again. Everyone else nodded. The matriarch began pounding her fist on her collarbone. The whole incident was taking on a distinctly funereal cast. Surely the mere decamping of a tradesman was not worth all this evident anguish.

I had a sudden vision of a carpenter, overalls bloodstained, workbelt loosened, his body surrounded by 10-penny nails, lying dead in the television room.

We entered the house; we walked down the long dark hall to the den in back. There was discordant harpsichord music playing in my head. Had I stumbled onto a blood feud with its roots high in the Hindu Kush? I entered the television room cautiously. No bodies.

I looked at the daughter. "Your carpenter was here?" I asked, gesturing vaguely around the room.

"No, no. I here." Her tone indicated more than a little impatience.

"Then where was the carpenter?"

"Carpenter gone," she said. Silly question.

We moved back to the living room. "Carpenter here," she said. She marked the place on the floor with her foot. Her grandmother indicated another place about eight feet away.

"Carpenter," she said.

Another image swam into my brain: a gigantic carpenter, a behemoth of an artisan, crawling on his belly like a reptile across the living room floor; a carpenter on a bad acid trip, thrashing about like a beached porpoise.

But why were they all so sad to be rid of this alarming spectacle? And, in any event, what was I supposed to do about it?

"We are not communicating," I said, moving my thumb and fingers in opposition, as though imitating the quacking of a duck. They looked at me as though I were mad.

"Kabul," said the grandmother, adding a new and bewildering element. The carpenter from Kabul is gone. It sounded like some sort of spy code.

The daughter got down on the floor and stretched her arms out. "Carpenter here," she said. "Now gone." Somehow, that finally did it.

"Ohhhhhh," I said. "Your *carpet* is gone."

I was then able to piece the story together: They'd all been in the back watching TV and some bold thief with impeccable taste had walked in and stolen a large rug hand-woven in Kabul. Not good at all.

A few hours later, the daughter appeared at my door with a fuller explanation. An uncle, she said, had come in and borrowed the carpet; an uncle unfamiliar with the customs of his adopted nation. She would not meet my eyes when she told me this.

I definitely haven't ruled out the Hindu Kush blood feud theory.

REAL ESTATE TIPS

As I have now actually purchased actual real estate in a fine American city, I feel that I can share with readers the many lessons I have learned in this amusing commercial voyage toward a sounder tax position.

The first rule of home buying is: Anywhere you want to live you can't afford. That leaves the places you don't want to live. Select the one you don't want to live in least. This is your dream house.

Next it is time to make an offer. The current owner of the home (or seller, in real estate jargon) will have produced a fictional number that represents the selling price. The buyer (that's you) then provides an equally fictional number that represents the price the buyer is willing to pay.

This process is not without irony. The seller, who is trying to unload the house, praises it to the skies and values it highly. The buyer, who desires the house, does his best to indicate what a disgusting little hovel it is.

Then the buyer and the seller (frequently accompanied by anywhere from 2 to 16 real estate agents) drink many cups of coffee and say offensive things to each other in a calm and even tone of voice.

This is called negotiation.

At the end, a document with many many clauses is signed, and the real fun begins. You have entered Escrow.

Escrow is a concept straight out of Tolkien. It is a land of sea serpents and monsters, dark caves, endless plains, hags with snake hair, sudden explosions. All the elves and other friendly folk have long since been exterminated; you're on your own in Escrow.

At the edge of this uncharted territory, in a dank and foul-smelling cave, surrounded by simpering toads, lives the Title Company. In order to cross Escrow, you must pay a sum of money to the Title Company. The Title Company does nothing in exchange for this money, except agree not to kill you.

Soon after, no matter where you try to hide in Escrow, you will encounter the Termite People. The Termite People, you will have been warned, are all thieves. They will demand a large sum of money to come and "inspect" your new home.

This inspection typically consists of a Termite Person standing on your front lawn, gazing at your home and saying, "You've got a problem there." He then announces that for $10,000, he will seek appropriate remedies. The Termite People are the chosen minions of the Title Company, who use them to wage all-out war on its mortal enemy, the loathsome Powder Post Beetle. There has not been a Powder Post Beetle sighted in North America since the French and Indian Wars, but every year the Termite People nevertheless pretend to kill great quantities of them.

If they don't, the Title Company will force them to enter Escrow.

At the center of Escrow, on top of the highest mountain, where the dark clouds lower eternally, stands the Lending Institution. The Lending Institution has many names: sometimes it is called S&L, which stands for Slothful and Lethargic*; sometimes it is called a Bank, which stands for no craven excuses from the likes of you.

Whatever it's called, it will agree to lend you enough money to make up the difference between the "down payment" (which represents all the money you've been able to accumulate by eating table scraps and working nights at the toxic waste dump for 10 years) and the actual purchase price of your home, in exchange for your immortal soul and the still-beating heart of your first- born child.

And then it will want "points." Very simply, points are the insult that is traditionally added to injury.

After it has eaten the points, it will allow you to leave Escrow and enter your home, where you will soon discover 13 unusual facts about your plumbing. Too late to do anything about that; you wouldn't want to enter Escrow again.

You'd sooner take cold showers in the kitchen sink, and you will.

*Note eerily prescient sarcasm in this 1984 column

47

MY DIRT

Let's not get into why I needed the dirt. I just needed the dirt, that's all. There were other options, of course; we could have had the house suspended from the necks of flying pelicans, or filled all the walls with molten lead, but on balance dirt seemed to be the way to go.

First of all, I definitely couldn't use my own dirt. My backyard has a large and lovely assortment of dirt and dirtlike substances available for the prudent homeowner, but using those dirts would strip the topsoil and kill the weed boutique I have caused to spring up there.

I was offered instead the unique opportunity to buy dirt. In my innocence, I believed that dirt was basically a low-ticket item, a commodity that should be, yes, dirt cheap. It appears, however, that your high-grade dirt costs an ugly penny and a lot of folding money as well. Surely, I said to my dirt broker, it would be possible to find free dirt.

Turns out that covert trading in bartered dirt is tricky. Free dirt is available at certain construction sites, but it must be removed immediately. The dirt broker, his finger ever on the pulse of the shifting dirt option market, announced that he could probably obtain some free dirt. He would bring it over and dump it by the curb, he said, and then come back when he had a moment to take the dirt from the front of the house to its final resting place in the basement.

My wife and I conferred on the matter. We were hunched in the basement at the time with the dirt broker; we looked like three crapshooters in the middle of a singularly boring dice game. We decided to take our chances on the free dirt strategy.

Several days later, the broker called up with a glad cry clinging to his throat. "Got your dirt," he said. "Be right over." In a twinkling, a load of dirt the size of New Hampshire was dumped in front of the house. A large flatbed truck containing yet more dirt was parked next to the pile.

It was sort of pleasant in a way, staring out the front window at my dirt. Gives a man a solid feeling, knowing he's got a load of dirt to fall back on in rough times. Other people park their fancy new cars in their driveways; I could show off my dirt.

"Great lookin' loam you got there," Mr. Williams from down the street would say. "Ah-yup," I would say, kicking it stoutly with my toe.

The next day it rained.

Here is a fact of nature that has probably not escaped your attention: Water added to dirt produces mud. My wife got on the phone to the broker. In a trice—a 36-hour trice—he was over to put a plastic tarp over the dirt piles, now becoming mud piles, or pies.

This was in December. Remember December? It just rained and rained and rained. The soil broker couldn't transfer the dirt in the rain. That would involve removing the tarp, and the damn stuff was wet enough already, wasn't it? So there it sat through the dank gray days. The water leaked under the tarp and caused the bottom layer of dirt to adhere to the concrete. The wind lifted the corners of the tarp and spattered the sides of the pile with moisture. I began to think of the dirt as some character in a children's story—"The Little Pile That Got Lost in the Rain."

"Oh please, Mr. Cloud, go away and let my dirt get dry," I said, more than once. But Mr. Cloud didn't, and sometimes Mr. Anger would take up residence just behind my eyes.

But all things come to an end, and one day the sun came out and wheelbarrows arrived and the dirt was transferred to our basement. Then it was time to tamp down the dirt.

And this is my advice: Never ever get yourself in a situation where you have to supervise the tamping down of dirt.

HISOWNBADSELF, BABE ROOF!

Sometime last winter it was, wife and self were sitting around the house stuffing orphans into envelopes and mailing them to deserving families in Indiana, when we happened to notice a small sound just outside our front door.

"Plip," went the sound. And then: "plip."

"We have a plip," said my wife.

"Probably just the wind in the eaves," I said. "You know how it is in these gracious old mansions."

"Wind does not go plip," said my wife. "Wind goes whoosh." We looked at each other with doubt and trepidation. Something was amiss or, as we say these days, ams.

We went to the front door and opened it. We stared at the puddle on the porch. We stared at the water gathering on the ceiling or whatever you call the thing that covers the porch.

"Plip," went the water.

"Leak," went the husband.

The wife went something that it is forbidden to go in a family newspaper.

Months passed. It is of course not possible to fix the roof when it is raining, and it is of course possible to wrap some serious denial around a leaky roof in the sunny months. Then we had rain again; then we had reality.

On balance, reality is a poor substitute for watching football on television until your roof falls on your head. This is my opinion, anyway.

So we got an estimate: eight million dollars. Seems steep for a roof, even a steep roof, but the workers were all licensed baritones and would sing selections from George Gershwin as they worked.

We decided to low-ball it. We went to Convicted Felons R Us, a group of very pleasant young men who took a particular interest in our electronic equipment. "Whaddya think one of these babies would fetch?" a worker asked me, running his hand licentiously over my VCR.

We rejected them as well. It was a gut feeling kind of deal.

We decided to approach the matter sideways. We would first decide on what sort of roof covering we wanted. Things would sort themselves out from there, we were pretty sure.

I did so want to go to the retail establishment in person to select the possible coverings, but unfortunately I was watching football on television, that Rutgers-Princeton matchup I had been looking forward to with such keen anticipation. "Go, Tigers, go," I yelled with apparent conviction until my wife was safely in the car.

She returned with samples. They are called tiles, but they are not cute little colored squares. They are mammoth tarry things that smell like a longshoreman's breakfast.

After the arrangement comes the decision, as T. S. Eliot may have said in an early draft. Reading from left to right, there were the sandy tiles, the dusky tiles, the bland tiles, the boring tiles and the red tiles.

We stared at them together. I hate moments like that, because I know I'm supposed to think something, but nothing actually enters my head.

"The red tiles . . ." I said.

"They're a little much," said my wife

". . . are a little much," I said.

It came down to sandy versus dusky.

"The sandy tiles pick up the sandy colors," I said firmly.

"But the dusky tiles pick up the dusky colors," she said.

"You're probably right," I said. This is called a "working relationship." All is agreement and harmony in the home right now and tomorrow the men will come to gouge my house apart.

A modern marriage is like a modern home, but I forget why.

THE RETURN OF BABE ROOF

No, see, because my old office at *The Chronicle* was right opposite a fire station and twice a day or so the doors would whomp open and the engines would come screaming out, and I pretty much got used to the noise. Also, there were accidents and demonstrations and I worked through them.

I laugh at distractions. Ha ha ha. I am a professional. Ha ha ha.

Also I am a spiritual being having a human experience and just because workmen are tearing off my roof and making my house tremble and creating HUGE BANGS every 30 seconds is as nothing to me, the professional.

It is part of having a new roof. Off goes the old roof; on comes the new roof. I can understand, now there are pieces of roof falling past my window. Like little dead birds, they are, falling falling and then crashing crashing into the garden.

The daylily; there. I did not like that daylily as much as some of my other plants. What after all is one daylily in the great scheme of things? I have seen nature LORD oh yes well, of course when debris hits the dumpster there's bound to be a teensy little clang.

But that is not the important part. What is the important part? I seem to have forgotten for just a second what the important part is.

Well, the new roof, silly me. It will be a nice color and repel water and are they wearing metal boots up there or what? No problem. I laugh at distractions.

So I have been into the kitchen and the stove is singing. Yes, so entirely competent am I at stress management that I've decided I need MORE CAFFEINE to help me through this little dilemma. I am a working professional. I profess that I work. I am babbling, but not really.

Apparently they have a radio up on the roof although how they can hear the damn thing is beyond me with all the NOISE, but they have the radio leaned up against the stove vent and the sound comes down into the kitchen.

My stove is playing a radio station called The Rocker. My stove is playing 16 in a row. My stove is playing really hot music. That is one of the jokes I am so famous for: stove, hot music, and so forth. I have the ability to find the drainpipe in anything. Former drainpipe. Didn't need it anyway. They probably intended to do that. Gosh I hope it doesn't rain. I really hope that.

So now this is an amusing twist. I cannot get out my back door.

There is a lot of debris on the back porch so the door will not open and that's more or less that. This is temporary, of course.

It is very important to me that it be temporary. I do not want half a ton of soggy debris on my back porch after the rains come, which of course they won't but what if they, now what? They're running around with some sort of tarp.

I get it. They're going to hurl really a lot of ex-roof into the garden and they want to protect the garden. A charming sentiment; on the other hand a lousy tarp is not going to protect a hyacinth shoot from a DIRECT HIT by a giant shingle.

Oh my, look at that. They're putting a tarp over the neighbors' yard, too. We got on so well with those neighbors. "The roof has gotta go somewhere." They have said this and who can argue? I wonder whether the neighbors would like a jar of jam or something. Sorry about your yard and have some preserves; so homey, so American.

As a professional, I look on the bright side. This is my training.

One day I shall die: That is the bright side.

A SMALL GIRL WALKING BACKWARD

It was a nice day and I was strolling, just strolling, down a sidewalk in charming yet frequently maligned Oakland, a city in California. And I saw a girl walking backward.

She was, at a guess, 10 years old. Her concentration was total. The tip of her tongue was peeking out of the corner of her mouth. She was looking down; novice backward walking does require attention to the feet.

She was walking backward up the sidewalk. She was walking backward with complete intention and attention.

She was, in a sense, conducting an experiment. Because I did not speak to her, I don't know the exact parameters of the experiment, but it was something like: How far can I walk backward without running into something or tripping or otherwise embarrassing myself?

This is what kids do; they perform experiments.

They are trying to figure out how the world works, and adults haven't been all that much help. If you ask your mom how far a human being can walk backward without falling into the ocean or winding up in China, she will say, "You shouldn't walk backward. You might hurt yourself."

Scientifically speaking, this is not a useful sentiment. Kids do not want considered opinions; they want facts. This girl was doing what scientists do: She had formed a hypothesis and was engaged in testing it. Kids are natural experimenters; they enjoy unexplained results.

My own kidhood was filled with experiments. I wanted to know whether a bike could jump a curb without substantial damage to the rider. The answer, as it happened, was no, but the validity of the experiment was confirmed by independent experts.

Later, I wanted to discover whether it was possible to leap into a compost pile from the top of a garden shed. My current survival indicates that this act did not violate the known laws of physics. This was an extremely comforting outcome to me personally; my Alive

Quotient (AQ) remained steady no matter how often I hurled myself, in a state of bliss and rage, off the roof of the shed.

During that same period, I sought to discover whether (a) it was possible to find every Elmer Valo baseball card ever issued, (b) it was possible for the average American youth to burn harmless spiders without also adversely impacting the floor and (c) it was possible for the average American youth to say the words "Prince Albert in a can" into a telephone without being arrested.

The answers were (a) no, (b) no and (c) yes.

So when I saw the girl walking backward, I thought about the scientific nature of childhood. No one had told her to walk backward; no one had suggested that this would be a nice thing to do for school or an appropriate topic of conversation for the family dining table.

She was doing what she was doing because she required knowledge. She did not have a grant or a salary or the promise of a Nobel Prize. She was in pursuit of pure knowledge. It was not that she was planning to walk backward for the next 30 years; it was that she wanted to know what would happen if somebody (not her) made that decision.

In an ideal society, these experimental urges would be gently harnessed in institutions of primary education. Not happening right now, worse luck. But we still have small girls walking backward.

WHERE THE RUBBER MEETS THE LAWN

I do not myself own a lawn mower. This is not because I am lazy or cheap; I'm sure that you, my friends, understand that. No, my failure to own a lawn mower has to do with my unswerving commitment to building a sense of community in my neighborhood.

It was just last weekend, in fact, after the UPS man complained about almost being trampled by the herd of wildebeest living in the grass under my front window, that I strode forth into the neighborhood to borrow a lawn mower.

Before it was over, I had interacted in a positive, community-building way with Diane and Noel and Ashley and Gracie and Ed, all authentic neighbors. Of course Diane lives next door so I interact with her pretty regularly anyway, and Noel is Diane's sister so I see her a lot, and Ashley is five-something and Gracie is one-something, so that pretty much leaves Ed as the significant interaction object.

Still, it was a fine moment. Bonds of trust were established. "Here you go," said Ed, rolling the lawn mower up his driveway. "Thanks," I said courteously. (Courtesy builds trust.) Later, I said, "Thanks" and Ed said, "No problem." It was a guy thing. You wouldn't understand.

It is interesting to me, in the litany of male-dominated activities, how few women are really interested in breaking the lawn mower barrier. You hardly ever hear a woman say, "This country will never truly be equal until we see women out there on Sunday afternoons mowing the lawns of America."

You rarely see lawn mowing listed as one of the necessary skills an independent woman should possess. Auto repair, checkbook balancing, plumbing, carpentry; all of these have taken on an aura of desirability. But lawn mowing? I have yet to see a self-help book titled *Yes! You Can Mow the Lawn!*

Not that women don't mow lawns. Many women do. It's just that you never hear any of them say, "One good thing about being alone: I finally get to mow the lawn my way."

Lawn mowing is Robert Bly heaven. Iron John, mower of lawns. Beat the drums, strip to the waist, lock up the children; it's time to cut us some grass.

It's more than New Age; it's patriotic. As I stood with 32 pounds of throbbing metal at the end of my fingers, ready to cut a wide swath, I felt like an American husband and father, a homeowner, a taxpayer, a citizen.

I have a lot of trouble feeling like an American. I tend not to believe the things Americans are supposed to believe. Americans are always someplace else, doing something else; our paths rarely cross.

Particularly American men. I have seen American men at the park, at the BART station, in line at Disneyland. They do not look like me, or anyway they do not look the way I think I look. I am visited with the suspicion that they do not think the way I think either. (American men are distinct from my friends. My friends aren't American men either. We are Martian men, spending a little time away from home planet.)

But with a lawn mower in my hands, surrounded by suburban sights and smells, walking up and down my front yard in orderly rows, I felt like an insider again. I was living in my own country as a citizen; I was living on my own block as a guy.

Fathers mowing lawns with sons; oh beautiful for spacious skies. A double epiphany in less than half an hour, plus a neatly trimmed lawn.

Ed! Ed's mower! What a life.

JUST WHAT I NEED: A CONCRETE DWARF

Well, it comes to this. You think you're just killing a few weeds and replacing them with half a dozen low-maintenance shrubs, and the next thing you know you're involved with drainage and bulb-splitting and pruning theories and enlightened pest management and fertilizers identified only by a series of numbers—"throw some of that 0-10-10 along the back fence."

Nor is that the worst. At a certain point, the whole notion of garden ornaments begins to seep into your life.

Garden ornaments.

I am not actually involved with garden ornaments.

According to my life plan, I am now an impoverished poet living in North Beach. My work is published in small stapled volumes and rarely reviewed. Lawrence Ferlinghetti calls me by name when we meet in coffee houses.

"Jon," he says, "loved that Nixon thing."

Bartenders and whores (the two job classifications from which I draw the majority of my friends) love my cynical, world-weary view of life, my mordant quips about the Establishment. My wife dresses entirely in black and makes herbal poultices in her spare time. I am personally acquainted with jazz musicians and Enrico Banducci.

I read the bulletin board at City Lights. "Mimi and Francie need cross-country ride week of 7/21." M&F can count on me; I frequently drive across the country. I'm a Dharma bum.

I know a great deal about haiku and medieval tapestries. I know nothing whatsoever about garden ornaments.

And yet, how amusing are the unexpected twists of life! Just last weekend, I found myself in Mendocino with my wife (who knows nothing of poultices, herbal or otherwise) strolling among the itsy-bitsy cutesey-wootsy boutiques and discussing something other than haiku, about which we know little.

We encountered a shop (perhaps a shoppe) called "London Frog." I found the name to be an amusing pun. I suggested that we tarry for a few moments in the friendly (and warm) confines of said retail establishment.

London Frog specializes in garden ornaments. Concrete gulls, metal ducks, heads of the Buddha, sundials, snails, dwarves, you-name-it. And I found myself thinking, all unbidden: Gee, one of those little things sure would be funny in our garden.

Unexpected and peculiar, I thought. Just the thing, I thought.

I was surprised at my own thoughts; on my impoverished poet's salary, I can scarcely afford groceries, much less a concrete dwarf.

I turned to my wife. "Wife," I said, "how about one of these lovely concrete snails, a steal at just $18?"

"You really think so?" she asked. The simultaneous translator of happily married life whispered in my ear: "Over my dead body."

We left the store and strolled out to the headlands. We discussed the underlying theories of garden ornaments. I suggested that, like some Mendocino residents, we could nail discarded hubcaps to the outside of our home.

We decided that we wouldn't do that either. We gazed at two red-billed oyster catchers plucking disconsolately at the rocks. I mumbled something.

"What?" asked my wife.

"We are the people our parents wanted us to become," I said.

"Too true," she said.

MOMENTS OF APPROPRIATE JOY

So I am sitting in Carrara's, the Emeryville restaurant famed for its polenta, eating said polenta and thinking about nothing in particular. There are high windows along the south wall of Carrara's, and an avalanche of sun is pouring through them, and I think, in that clever way I have: sun.

Not that anemic winter light, smelling of dentures and disease, old gray fragile sun lying exhausted on the rooftops, but the authentic article, polenta-colored sun, thick as honey, rolling down the walls, puddling on the floor, excessive and hot: that sun.

Say spring? Yes indeed. Say spring.

It's been a confusing winter, with the apocalypse followed by the rain followed by announcements that we shouldn't take the rain too seriously followed by razor-sharp air and chunky sun.

Here's how to tell if it's spring: Just take your egg beaters out of the sun. If it peaks, you've got spring.

If you peak, you've got spring.

I might be getting just the teeniest bit giddy in here.

So I am standing on a suburban street corner with two large books about baseball under my arm. Two books about baseball: That would be a leading seasonal indicator. If the sun is as thick as polenta, and you are carrying two books about baseball under your arm, it may very well be spring.

I am looking through a chain-link fence at a vacant lot, an urban space that was once a building and then a parking lot and now a terrace of cracked concrete elaborately protected for insurance reasons.

And in the middle of this littered heath, rising from a small crack in the pavement, is one daffodil.

A daffodil is not a weed. It is not widely propagated by the wind or the birds. Someone must have planted this daffodil. Maybe before the fence was put up; maybe not. But at some point someone took a look at this discouraging landscape and said, "You know, what this place needs is a daffodil."

It looks pretty plucky, that daffodil. It looks pretty hopeful. The sun is dripping down the walls and finds the cracks in the pavement, and the sun-colored daffodil is standing like a prairie dog in a warm wind, and I am seized with this odd desire to sing.

So I am kneeling in my garden and the sun is still raining like polenta and the radio is playing the music of baseball and I am digging into the dirt and I am smelling: chocolate.

These would be your cocoa bean hulls. They make good mulch; they're rich in Seven Important Somethings; they smell like chocolate. Really like chocolate. When you get at nose level with cocoa bean hulls, there's not a lot happening in your sensory panorama except chocolate.

The hulls have been sitting in plastic bags in the sun, so they're warm to the touch. Bathwater temperature, say. So I am down underneath the rhododendron bush (which is doing something outrageous with pink) with my hands wrist-deep in hot chocolate and the sun on my back and a sharply hit ground ball in my ear and this feeling that might very well be joy begins to make my eyes water.

Hel-lo. Nice to have you back. Take a seat in my cerebellum and stay as long as you want.

Things are indeed terrible all over. This is a known fact. What is not generally acknowledged is that things are also not terrible all over.

THE GARDEN OF AMBIVALENCE

For those keeping score, the first daffodil of the 1989 season opened at precisely 8:13 A.M. on Friday, February 24, in that little spot between the path and the magnolia bush.

It was followed by the first hyacinth of the 1989 season, which elbowed a daylily leaf out of the way at precisely 4:32 P.M. on Saturday, February 25. The fact that the hyacinth was planted that close to the daylily led to an interesting exchange between the garden copresidents.

I am aware that other bulb-induced plants may have appeared in other locations prior to the dates noted above. But, quite frankly, who cares? Let them get their own newspaper columns.

In other areas of the garden, the tulips are pushing their clever way up through the soil, the magnolia is already in full bloom and the hellebores continue to amaze. The artichoke is up slightly in light trading.

One rhododendron has popped. I wish I knew which one, but the little stakes with the names on them got buried in mulch about two years ago so I don't know what to call any of my rhodos except "Mrs. Betty Robertson."

Non-gardeners will think I'm joking, but I'm not. I also have a plant called dropmore purple, but that's another story and not a very good one.

Yes, and of course there's the datura and the *Sparmannia africana*, two of my favorite plants, both of which look as though they'd been subjected to several years of radiation treatments. They look like a symbol for all that is withered and diseased in the world.

Welcome to gardening ambivalence.

It really is a serious drag ("a serious drag"—you can take the boy out of the '60s but you can't take the '60s out of the boy) to walk out in the garden in early spring, the time of maximum joy, the time when all the labors of fall and winter are rewarded with beauty so heartbreaking and breathtaking that life seems whole again, and see five or six plants that look like something out of a horror movie.

It was that damn frost, of course. I know the snow looked pretty on Mount Tam, but it sure messed up a lot of gardens.

And the worst part is we can't even perform cosmetic surgery. "What," ask the alarmists, "if another frost comes? Then the tender buds will be exposed to the crew-ell winds of winter!"

"Snow on Mount Tam twice in one year?" I ask.

"What do you know?" they respond. Gardeners, as mentioned above, tend toward overweening arrogance. When you're dealing with plants, you need every defense mechanism you can find.

So all these dead bodies, all these hanging trees waiting for a rope, have to loom over my garden until April Fool's Day. The little tulips must needs look up and see their fate spread above them. It's sort of like having the Ghost Of Christmas-Yet-To-Come take up root near your back fence.

Gardening is like being a Giants fan; it's always a wait-till-next-year proposition. If it ain't the frost, it's the scale, or the red spider mites. There are only partial victories, temporary triumphs.

I suppose, for those with sufficient peace of mind to handle the whole thing, there's something to be said for eternally being reminded of the skull beneath the skin. There are no illusions in the garden, and it's useful to realize that beauty is just as real as death.

NOT EXACTLY LIKE EDEN

In March and April, they were just as perfect and lovely as a photograph in a seed catalog. But now it is May, and their flowers have withered and tumbled, and the bulb greens are flopping on the ground, leaning limply against one another, like drunken soldiers whose general has been relieved of command.

I can't cut them because while they are lounging in the dirt they are passing nutrients to their bulbs far below, so I just rubber-band them together in neatish bundles.

It's tedious work, without true function; even silly.

My mind kicks over slowly, an engine on idle. Idle hands are the devil's playground. Is that right? An idol's hands are the devil's playground. A mind on idle is the devil's playground.

Most garden speculations tend to start, however vaguely, with some notion about the relationship of garden tasks to the larger world of living beings.

Sometimes it gets real grim real quick. Once you've spent some time in the garden, you realize in a specific and incontrovertible way that life on the planet would be a lot better if there were about half as many people around.

If a garden stays the same size and the number of plants increases exponentially . . . well, you can do certain things short-term to alleviate the problem, but pretty soon you're going to have to start killing plants.

If you don't, then the plants will start killing each other. And the ones you like will be the first to go. (Maybe that's why you like them; fragility, like rarity, is highly prized.) So, since you are a god to your delphiniums, you pluck and maim according to your own inscrutable tastes.

That's why man invented the concept of weeds. A weed is just a plant you don't like; it has neither more nor less inherent virtue than any other plant.

The question is: Does God believe in weeds?

And are you one?

Enough. The sense of omnipotence is bogus in any event. Your garden has a vote as well; you reach a compromise based on respective energy levels. (Time is not an issue; the garden always has more time.)

Blackberries, oxalis, morning glories, Bermuda grass—you do not win battles with these relentless vegetables; you just decide on a level of mutual accommodation. The morning glory can have the back fence unless and until it should snake out a tendril toward the roses, in which case cometh the terrible swift shears.

(I sometimes envision signing these concords in a large sunny room filled with Louis XIV furniture; me on one side of the table, the purple-headed morning glory wrapped around an armchair on the other, bending over the document, a pen clutched in its vine.)

But eternal vigilance is the price of liberty. Turn your back, and zap—the Spanish lavender is devoured by Bermuda grass. And then, in fearsome retaliation, you exact revenge upon the vile weed; sort of a coup de grass.

In other words, it's the international arms race out beyond the screen door. The allegorical lessons of this mini-balance-of-terror do not exactly fit with liberal orthodoxy, but maybe the comparisons are inexact.

Or maybe not.

It's not our animal natures we have to worry about, it's the way in which we too closely resemble plants.

THE VOLUNTEERS ARE AT THE GATES!

It's pretty much of a big nothing in the garden this time of year. A few penstemon are still blooming; the iochroma and the lavatera are pumping out flowers; but most of the plants have adopted a wait-and-see attitude. Our perennials may be hardy, but they are not boastful.

We have a tomato plant that still has green tomatoes on it; we have a tomato plant that is apparently still growing, sprawling over the lavender, but we are ignoring it. We planted it at the right time; we harvested it at the right time; if it wants to pretend it's still September, that's its problem.

The Early Girl has become an elderly bawd; we do not speak of it in front of the children.

Mostly there is leaf removal and weeding. A garden is, alas, not a lawn; you can't just get the great rake and round up the dogies. A more primitive technology is involved, the technology of the human back bending and the human hand grasping.

The magnolia, the apple and the persimmon are the worst offenders. They seem to drop twice as many leaves as they had on their branches. It's one of those wonders of nature.

The weeds are quite amazing. They seem to sense that this is a good time to take root, when the other plants are quiescent and the gardeners are inattentive. We have learned to identify the familiar kinds—we don't know their names; we just remember them from the previous cycle—but each year there are newcomers.

There's a nice name for these newcomers: volunteers. Mostly volunteers are just another variety of weed, because that is why weeds are weeds. Their seed is widely scattered; they live in any kind of soil; they are rude to other plants.

Weeds are slatterns; the Early Girl would be a weed were it not for its fruit. When a weed gives good fruit, we forgive its wandering ways, at least for a time. There is a nice metaphor here, but this column had not planned to go in that direction.

The tomato is not a volunteer; we planted it. It's the unfamiliar things that we didn't plant that pose a dilemma just now. We stare at these odd green shoots, we mush-brained suburbanites somehow invested with the power of life and death in our plant kingdom, wondering whether this volunteer should be allowed to flourish.

Sometimes we have said yes, and regretted it. Acacia is a tenacious guest, fast-growing, deeply rooted and reluctant to leave. We had some weird pineapplelike plant under the camellia last year that threatened most of central Oakland before we dismissed it. Still, I like the idea of volunteers. I like the notion that my backyard is not so far removed from nature that wandering seeds and spores cannot find my carefully amended soil.

It's a poignant, lovely notion: the unseen, wind-borne universe of reproduction. Millions of questing eggs, lighter than dandelion fluff, hurled up to the clouds, pushed across rivers and rocks, finally finding a shelter, water, food, a blanket of soil.

And then, sooner rather than later, the seed breaks, the shoots start, and within a few weeks the suburbanites are staring down. "Are you a something?" ask the yard-owners. The volunteer remains mute but tries to look exotic, medicinal, ripe with the possibility of fragrance.

So they remain. Not much going in the garden anyway; a little experimentation can't hurt. When the enfranchised foliage starts, there'll be another census taken.

Some winnowing will occur. Vulgar flowers will stay; unusual foliage will stay. The rest will become compost, rich with promise, home to the next generation of volunteers.

HOW TO COMBAT THAT BULBY FEELING

Sheer absolute madness. True lunacy. Horticultural weirdness that surpasseth human understanding. And I am in the dark swirling center of it, experiencing the vertigo that is available only to those who have at last taken leave of their senses.

It is (as Jack Webb used to say) 6 P.M. on a November Saturday. I am working the loam beat out of Backyard Station. It is dark. I am down on my hands and knees. A flashlight is beside me on the ground, throwing giant shadows against the rear wall of my home.

I am digging in the earth. My hands are cold; my knees are sore; my back is sending me brisk telegrams: "Don't Try To Stand Up Stop I Am Locked In This Position Forever Stop Please Stop Stop."

And yet I continue. Beside me, in a limp cardboard box, are a large number of small brown objects. They look like onions rejected by sensible shoppers, or worse.

Chimpanzee leavings. Gnome scat.

Bulbs.

I am placing these bulbs in the ground. I am nestling these ugly spheres in a tablespoon of expensive bone meal. I am covering the spheres with good rich earth. I have been performing this act for five hours. Also my wife has been performing this act. Also my younger daughter. Also Jim, the Bulb Broker. Four people devoting five hours to plunging dwarf coprolites into the ground.

I absolutely refuse to tell you how many bulbs I purchased. Wild horses would be insufficient to drag that number from me. OK: 1150. You heard me: one thousand, one hundred and fifty bloody stupid bulbs.

Iris, tulips, daffodils, lilies, more. Names like "Royal Blush" and "Scarlet Lady" and "Winter Princess." The monetary equivalent of the gross national product of Albania, invested in stunted leeks and buried in my backyard.

Time was, earlier, when I bought plants. Plants are swell. They look like something a person would want to buy. They have leaves and stems. Sometimes they even have flowers. They spruce up a garden immediately.

In the morning, you can go out and look at your plants. Oooh, another leaf. A little bud. Good going, guys.

Bulbs, on the other hand. . . . The next morning, after my nocturnal planting orgy, I hobbled down to the garden in the posture generally associated with servants named Igor. I stared at the ground.

Two earthworms and a half-buried trowel. Are we having photosynthesis yet? We are not.

****

Ah, but that was then and this is now. This very morning, my back as good as new, I strode into that very same garden. I looked at that very same earth. Shoots.

All over the place, shoots. With great courage, having pushed their way through the adobe compound that forms the soil around my home, the shoots are poking their heads into the brisk air.

They look perky; they look happy. If you put your ear next to them, you can almost hear them singing about the flowers they will some day extrude.

It's January, and spring has come to Oakland. The earth has been renewed; the inevitability of vegetation has been reaffirmed; a dozen cheap poems are being written even as I speak.

Good old gnome scat.

PACIFIC OVERTURES: A LESSON IN SAND

A sand painting is a tidy metaphor; almost too tidy. Seems like Buddhism 101; a catechism for the young monks. Why do we paint with sand? To show the beauty in the humblest things. Why do we destroy the painting? To show the impermanence of all things.

So the Tibetan monks, duly blessed by the Dalai Lama and Richard Gere, began to create a sand painting at the Asian Art Museum in Golden Gate Park. It was their plan to make the painting and then, in a grand ceremony, to destroy it and hurl the grains into the sea, as is their custom.

(Perhaps not precisely their custom, as access to beachfront property in Tibet is severely restricted, but one limitless natural feature can stand for another. It's a walk-on part; the ocean has no lines.)

And then a crazy lady came and messed up the painting before the monks got a chance to mess it up themselves, and no one knew how to feel. The monks just nodded and went to lunch, a very satisfactory response and duly noted as such.

It was destined to be destroyed anyway; where was the crime? But that same argument could be used to justify any act of violence. It will all be destroyed one day anyway; why are we quarreling over timing? And yet timing is everything, maybe the only thing; the question about death is never whether but when.

So it made a nice addition to the lesson. Within the planned impermanence is the unplanned impermanence. We can exercise and watch our diet and die when an anvil falls from the sky. This is not new information; none of it is new information.

They're always the same lessons; it's just when and how they're told. Timing is everything.

The part I always hated about gardening was the sand-painting part.

I always wanted the garden to stay put, at least for a little while, just remain for a few weeks in this configuration so I could get to know it, organize it in my mind, revel in it.

But it doesn't; it won't. If I try to force it to stop, it will die—it will choke on its own abundance, victimized by my refusal to keep my part of the bargain.

I can make some decisions; I can play God, moving the iris to a more advantageous location, pulling up the stipa before it goes to seed so its little daughters do not run amok amidst the ixia and the dianthus.

All this has to be done while it's still beautiful. A good gardener—I am not a good gardener, but I know some—can see into the future, can see what will murder what, what will die of too much sun or too much shade.

So much of gardening feels like destroying: pruning, transplanting, coping with pests, clearing out underbrush, dividing, furrowing the soil. A garden is a sand painting destroyed in sections. You can choose the sections, or you can wait to have them chosen. It comes to the same thing.

And this winter's hard frost was the crazy lady, the unplanned impermanence in the middle of the planned impermanence, a reminder that even our planned chaos is insufficient to cope with the real chaos beyond.

Nature, screaming about CIA and illicit radio transmissions, came and kicked the garden around. Had we been smart, we would have nodded and gone to lunch. We didn't; lessons repeated are not lessons learned.

The monks are making another painting now; I like that, too. And I have made another garden, like the old garden but different. I can see the roses and columbine from my window, red and yellow, sure to die.

71

My Charming and Naughty Family

I MUST ARISE AND GO FAR AWAY NOW

The one thing I really wanted to do during my trip to Ireland was to stand near the Lake Isle of Innisfree and recite the William Butler Yeats poem concerning same.

My younger daughter was with me. I thought that this direct encounter with poetry might be instructive for her. "I owe it all," she would tell reporters later upon receiving the Nobel Prize for Literature, "to that moment on the banks of the Lough Gill when my late father read out loud those majestic words that still. . ." and so forth.

I had thought that Innisfree might be hard to find—it is, after all, a symbol of remote rural harmony—but Yeats is something of a cottage industry in county Sligo, and the way is clearly marked.

"Lake Isle of Innisfree," the sign said. "Danger: Traffic entering from right."

As we drove, my wife recited the poem, and the three of us discussed it. That took about 45 seconds; it's not what you call a poem rich in subtext.

"Sounds like Yeats needed a vacation," said my daughter.

"In the bee-loud glade," I said, quoting.

"If there are bees," said my daughter, "I'm not getting out of the car."

We followed the signs; we arrived at a stony parking area. County Sligo had thoughtfully provided toilet facilities for Yeats lovers. The day had been dank and wet; we were the only people there.

"Where's Innisfree?" asked my daughter.

I point to the earth. "See the bent grasses, indicative of those who have come before. It is the path to the viewing area. Thus, Innisfree is that inspirational isle to the right."

"There's another island over there," said my wife.

"Wrong direction and too small," I said. We tromped over the grass. We sank ankle-deep in muck.

"I can see it from here," said my daughter, retreating. I went a little farther. I opened my book. "I will arise and go now; and go to Innisfree, and a small cabin build there, of clay and wattles made."

"What?" shouted my daughter, on higher ground.

"Wattles," I yelled back. "Slender branches and reeds." I had looked it up.

I continued to read, gesturing at appropriate moments to the island. "And I shall have some peace there —"

"Where?" my daughter yelled.

"There," I said, pointing. "Where peace comes dropping god-dammit slow."

I finished the poem and slogged back to the car. As we drove back to the main road, my wife leafed through a guidebook. "Listen to this," she said. "The tiny Lake Isle of Innisfree. Tiny. It must have been that other one. You had the wrong island."

"It hardly matters," I said. "It's all symbolic. It's really the *idea* of islands that concerns the poet here."

My wife made a small noise in her throat.

"At least there weren't bees," said my daughter.

THE DADDY PROBLEM: AN EXAMINATION

Hers are 3 and 7 and mine are 18 and 22, so I was able to give my chum Cyn Wages a few tips from the world of advanced parenting.

She was concerned about boyfriends so I told her—my older daughter is reading this on her lunch hour and her heart stopped at the beginning of that sentence. She has long lived in dread of my using her social life as grist for my large and indiscriminate mill.

In the interests of continuing my relationship with my children, I will leave boyfriends entirely alone. See posthumous columns for a more complete discussion.

"There will come a time," I told Cyn, "when you are a profound embarrassment to your children. You just have to accept that."

"I can't believe this is going to happen to me," she said. I snickered an irritating snicker.

"I bet it will. For instance, if she has friends over to the house and you decide to leave them alone to have fun, she will later tell you that Corinne was totally mad that you ignored her. All the other parents, she will tell you, have something that resembles a plausible line of chatter.

"So the next time you will say to Corinne, 'how's school?' and Corinne will say 'fine' and only later will you learn that Corinne is totally sensitive about school and your question was in the worst possible taste.

"Eventually, your child will decide that the only sensible solution is for you to disappear into your bedroom before her friends come over. When you decline to participate in her plan, she will look skyward— 'see what I have to put up with?'—and say, 'Daaaaaddy. . . .' "

"Gives me the chills just thinking about it," said Cyn.

The worst part, I said, dropping out of quotation marks for convenience's sake, is that it becomes a self-fulfilling prophecy. Your daughter's feelings about your unsuitability so rattles you that you lose all social graces.

The first thing to go is your understanding of the intricate network of relationships that bind them together. You even confuse their names, which is easy since half of them are named Jennifer.

You develop a curious kind of false heartiness. You launch into long, pointless stories and listen to yourself in amazement. In short, you become just like your own parents.

"Gives me chills just thinking about it," said Cyn.

One time, I recalled, I gave a barbecue for some friends of my older daughter. It was to be in our backyard, which at that time was a weed library surrounding an ancient redwood picnic table.

I wanted it to go right. I was nervous that the barbecue wouldn't get hot enough soon enough, so I resolved to start early and use a lot of coals.

The coals got hot enough, oh my yes. The first hamburger bun I dropped on the grill caught fire and burned to a small black cinder.

The burgers likewise hissed and blackened in seconds. I was confused and helpless, a protoplasmic gob of former parent.

"Come and get it!" I yelled, the lunatic chef wreaking havoc.

The dear little ones lined up and got their burgers, sooty on the outside and cold on the inside, carbon sushi. They crammed themselves on the benches next to the table and ate, staring at the weeds.

I went upstairs and sat, head in hands. I am, I thought, providing work for a generation of psychiatrists yet unborn.

COLD HANDS, WARM HEART

The only year there was an icicle outside Rachel's window was the year her window was in Illinois. The family moved to Evanston in 1972; it moved back in 1973. Kind of a cultural exchange program.

Rachel, because she was the older of our two daughters, got the bigger room. That was not fair, but when the rooms are different sizes nothing is fair. She got the bigger room because she was . . . taller. She needed more room. That's as logical as anything else, which is to say: not logical at all.

The icicle fascinated both her and me; we were both California kids. We couldn't believe that an icicle could look so much like itself, so much like a cartoon. It looked magical. Elves on bicycles throwing icicles; that phrase kept running through my brain. I thought it was from an old children's song; turned out I made it up.

I didn't really know what to make of winter at all. I wasn't used to single-digit temperatures; the phrase "wind chill factor" had a deeply disturbing sound. I pictured orphans shivering in snowdrifts; I pictured maidens pursued by ravening wolves.

During the first blizzard of the season, Rachel got lost walking home from school. School was a block away.

Some of my memories of winter are better than that. I remember one morning when Shana and I were home alone; Shana was then three. I'm not sure where the others were; I just know it was the two of us, staring out the window at the new-fallen snow.

"I shall," I thought, "take my child for a walk down to the lake. She'll remember that all her life." This is a thought that young parents frequently think; usually it turns out not to be true. Kids are largely unsentimental; greeting card "moments" go right past them.

The noise in the cellar, now; the noise in the cellar they'll remember on their deathbeds.

So we bundled up and walked down to the shore of Lake Michigan, three blocks away. When we got to the park fronting the lake, we walked on fresh snow, so our footprints were the first to break the white crust. Sometimes I carried her; my footprints got deeper.

We stood on the edge of the lake, looking out at the almost invisible place where the water joined the sky, a shade of gray merging into another shade of gray, almost certainly invisible to the camera, so subtle it seemed to exist almost entirely in the mind.

I looked at my daughter thinking her daughter thoughts. I thought my father thought: If I can concentrate on this moment, remember every detail, I can keep it in my memory forever, available when needed, three-year-old Shana ankle-deep in snow beside the ghostly lake. I concentrated; it worked. It's still there; I can see it now.

Ten years later, Shana and I went to Hawaii together. I had a story to write and she had a grandmother to see. I stayed in a beachfront Waikiki hotel with a spectacular view of Diamond Head.

Shana was awed. "You know," I said, "if you concentrate on that view real hard, take a picture in your memory, you'll have it with you forever." She took me seriously; she knitted her eyebrows and stared.

I watched her concentrating. I can see her now, leaning over the railing of the balcony, collecting her own horizons, her own past.

Maybe one day she will tell a child how to make time stand still. Elves on bicycles throwing icicles; shades of gray; shades of grace.

DAUGHTERS

If she has anything to say about it, and she probably will, next year at this time my older daughter will be in Europe. In her last summer of adolescent freedom (before the more absolute and more proscribed freedoms of adulthood), she will be seeking the pleasures and lessons of a more elderly branch of American civilization.

Which means that this is the last summer that both of my daughters will be in residence. My younger daughter will be in residence for a few more years yet, but the familiar dual dynamic, two sisters under one roof exploring the possibilities of life without school, will have come to an end.

In a sense, this is the fulfillment of my dreams. We raise these precisely fabulous human animals so that they may take their places in the larger world beyond; so that they may leave our homes and find others; so that they may know more than we do, and do better than we have. They are the arrows and we are the bows; nothing is clearer than that.

There have been times when I have anticipated this moment avidly. I have prayed on many occasions that the emotional and financial burdens of children be lifted from me sooner rather than later; that all this backing and filling and hueing and crying be at an end so I can settle down for some uninterrupted conversation with some people of my own age, at my own level of fatigue.

And yet it came too soon. It's not even here yet, and it came too soon.

Lately, in the shank of the evening, I have been playing the home movies in my head. The birth of my older daughter was accompanied by ambiguous portents—my wife suddenly took sick and had to be rushed to the delivery room; an unusual thunderstorm raged outside, spewing lightning over Oakland; the only book I had to read during the birth event was a prose translation of Dante's Inferno.

Later, I was required to drive one or the other of the daughters to the very same hospital as they sat beside me pale and shaking from some vile virus or amok bacteria. I remember the waves of relief I experienced when the illnesses turned out to be less than life-threatening—often, on the ride home, I was paler and more shaken than my suddenly chipper child.

And there were the surprising conversations, often at inopportune moments, when I was allowed unexpected access to the developing soul of one of my daughters. I was asked questions I didn't think I could answer. I answered them anyway. It worked out.

I was better than I thought I was; fatherhood transforms the father; nature saves its best work for children.

I perceived, for the first time, my own mortality—these beings would outlive me—and my own immortality—these beings carried within them the memory of my existence. And their existence, and my relation to their existence, helped me understand my own parents.

Oh yes, I said to myself, I see. Got it, Mom. Not that easy.

Last Wednesday, I watched my older daughter get into a nearly new automobile and drive off down the street with my younger daughter beside her on the front seat.

Three days before, the state of California had officially declared that she was competent to drive a car. I endorsed the notion, although it seemed scarcely credible that a person who just yesterday was throwing mashed peas at the wall should now be legally operating a motor vehicle.

But her hand on the wheel was firm; her foot on the accelerator was sure and even. My younger daughter turned around in her seat and waved. I waved back. Go with God, I whispered to myself.

And come back.

TEENAGE MUTANT NINJA JERK

I am the person I warned my parents about. I remember that about every six months, and then I forget it again. One day, six months will pass, and I won't remember to remember it.

That'll be it: geezerdom.

So let me lay out the situation for you. It was Christmas Day 1990. Our Christmas Days tend to be long family affairs, starting with a healthy breakfast of forbidden food, moving through the present exchange ritual, taking a prolonged energy dip through the fragmented and peaceful afternoon, then picking up with a large dinner at which the events of the day are analyzed in some depth.

During the afternoon lull, some of the younger members of the group suggested that it might be fun to rent a videotape and slump in front of it. Fine, I said, meaning it.

They went out and returned. They had selected *Teenage Mutant Ninja Turtles*. The truth about me and *Teenage Mutant Ninja Turtles* is that I don't know enough about them to have an opinion. I know that they say "Cowabunga, dude" and like pizza. I know that they fight evildoers.

I know that some people fretted that the movie was covertly anti-Asian, and other people believed that the movie was too violent for tots, and that still others noted the irony that we should be celebrating artificial turtles while our real frogs are disappearing at a mysteriously accelerating rate.

Calvin Trillin once said that he had no opinion about where the best chili in Cincinnati could be found, but it interested him very much that people argued about it so passionately. All that interests me about the Ninja Turtles is that people find them interesting.

Yeah, but. The offending videotape entered the home, and the protojerk deep within every father came to the surface. I whined, I sniveled. I remarked that *Rear Window* might have been a better choice.

81

Friends, *Rear Window* was made 37 years ago. It's as though, I told myself later, I had in my youth brought home a copy of *Invasion of the Body Snatchers* only to have my parents complain that they saw no reason why the whole family couldn't enjoy *Wings*.

Now, remember, I know little about these turtles. I am going entirely on rumor and nostalgia. *Rear Window* might be a better movie, but how would I know? And what criteria am I using, beyond free-floating grumpiness?

It feels almost tribal, almost genetic; the old guy sitting in the cave saying, "Obsidian arrow points? Well, excuse me, we never had any obsidian arrow points, and we managed to slaughter field rodents just fine."

It was always thus; I know it was always damn thus. I just can't imagine what it's doing inside my own brain. It's not like me. I don't do knee-jerk snobbish reactions to pop culture artifacts; I'm on the other side of that argument.

Except when my kids do it, in which case I remember that I used to walk nine miles through the pouring rain just to read one paragraph of Tolstoy. I didn't need *Teenage Mutant Ninja Turtles* because I was too busy . . . well, I was too busy looking for back copies of *Swank* magazine, but that was different.

That was me; this is them.

Perhaps this is a necessary social function. Perhaps reactionary, illogical parenting helps make the species stronger, helps the progress of humankind. It gives the young ones steel and fire; it trains them for the larger battles ahead.

That must be it. I don't want to be a grumpy cartoon dad; I'm just doing it for the children.

THE FLYING TRAPEZE

I recently had what you might call a situation, a narrative, concerning myself and my younger daughter, Shana, and feats of daredevil abandon every day except Monday and twice on Saturday. It was your terror and glory kind of deal; your dilemma of parenthood in rather starker and more vivid terms than usual.

Just over a year ago, Christmas of 1988, Shana was unemployed and I was still serving as a board member for the Pickle Family Circus, a nonprofit touring troupe of skilled performers to which I have, apparently without my volition, become attached.

The Pickles had a temporary opening for a box office manager; Shana had a permanent availability in her schedule. She was 18 at the time, and had ruled out only dentistry as a possible career goal. She took the job.

Naturally, the amusements of fate being what they are, Shana caught a severe case of the circus flu. She had found her place in the universe. She was accepted as a performing apprentice for the 1989 touring edition of the Pickle Family Circus.

Not that it mattered much, but I was in favor of the job. It seemed like a great life experience. She saw a lot of small and large towns up and down the Pacific Coast, she got strong and tan and supple, she learned to live cooperatively with a bunch of eccentric, friendly, impoverished performers and technicians.

Onstage, a performing apprentice's tasks are not overly rigorous. Shana appeared in the ensemble numbers, ran about zanily at the right times, and jumped onto one end of the teeterboard so the acrobat at the other end could fly into the air.

Many times, she raised her hand and gestured toward the center of the ring, smiling in that demented circus way. From my point of view it was sweet, a kind of After-School Special.

Then, in November, the aerialist left the circus. There was a meeting. Eyes swiveled slyly to Shana. Could she, they wanted to know, learn the act in three weeks? Sure it was tough, sure it was sudden, but . . . you're going out there a scared little kid and coming back a star.

Now then, play the parent. Your daughter says, "Daddy, I'm going to be the star aerialist!" That would be aerialist as in gymnastics 15 feet above the ground, as in death spirals and backward half-something and the Curse of the Flying Wallendas, as in Tinker Bell and ultimate freedom and every little girl's fantasy.

"Oh good!" you say, meaning: Oh no! "I have no control over this," you say, meaning: I've got to find a way to get control over this. "Is that thing safe?" you ask, meaning: That thing is not safe.

Her first scheduled public performance, her maiden opening night, was the premier event of the entire season, the grand opening at the Palace of Fine Arts in San Francisco, the annual holiday show that nets the Pickles 60 percent of their earned income and 80 percent of their publicity.

Part of the fantasy, of course, opening at the Palace, but part of the pressure too. Reality was immediately heightened; ordinary objects seemed to glow and waver.

Rehearsals were held at the converted church on Potrero Hill that serves as the Pickles' world headquarters; I decided not to go. I pretended I was doing that for Shana, so as not to put any more pressure on her, but the truth was that I was doing it for myself. I did not want to embarrass myself by screaming "my daughter, my daughter!" like some grieving peasant woman at the site of a Mediterranean aircraft disaster.

It was easy enough to read the rehearsal schedule and not wander in at the wrong time. It was less easy to predict how the rehearsal schedule would change. As it happened, the two collided. As it happened, I was seated on a hard bench on a cold, dark afternoon in the high-vaulted rehearsal room when Shana tried her act before the entire company for the first time.

Shana was performing what's called a cradle act. There is no trapeze, no swinging bar. Rather, there is a fixed rectangle of sturdy metal piping rigged 20 feet above the ground.

Shana was partnered with Jean-Luc Martin, a well-bicepsed French Canadian who had done the act with the previous aerialist. The act had three sections: First, Jean-Luc hung by his knees from the cradle and held Shana while she did tricks in the air, then the positions were reversed and Shana did the holding. Finally, Shana put a loop of rope around her neck and another around her ankles and then, suspended at these two points, face upward, held by Jean-Luc, she spun.

Can you visualize that? Daughter supine, 10 feet above the ground, suspended by a rope, rotating. Not exactly the same as daughter taking her history midterms at Bennington.

And the rehearsal did not go well. The music, written for the other act, was wrong. Soon the band stopped playing entirely, and the performers continued in silence, sometimes grunting softly. It was all sweat and muscle and concentration; no glamour at all.

They worked too fast; even I could see that. They seemed desperate.

At one point, Shana poked Jean-Luc in the eye. After it was over, he stood on the cradle with his palm over his eye, looking grim. Shana stood on the mat below, crying.

I did not know what to do. My urge was to go to her, but I was aware that she was, in some senses anyway, an adult who was having problems at the office, not a kid who had skinned her knee.

Finally, I sort of sidled over and hugged her. I said something comforting and brief. I walked out of the church feeling particularly lonely and pointless. That night, Shana and I talked on the phone for an hour, and I felt close again, and useful. The worst is over, I thought.

But the worst was not over.

Cut to December ninth, 24 hours before her opening-night debut at the Palace of Fine Arts. Dress rehearsal, more or less. I had been asked to write a few jokes for the show. I arrived about one in the afternoon, bearing cookies and soft drinks and a positive attitude.

The stage manager greeted me. "Has anyone talked to you yet?"

"You're the first," I said.

"Shana's fine," she said. The remark was meant to be comforting, but somehow it did not comfort.

"Why shouldn't she be?" I asked.

"We had to take her to the hospital. She'll be back in a little while. She, I guess, well . . . the truth is, she almost hung herself."

Remember the part of the act with the rope and the two nooses? The tricky part, as you might expect, is the dismount; Shana has to slip the rope over her neck at just the right moment.

During warm-ups, something went wrong. For a moment, the full weight of her body was borne by the rope around her neck. It could have been instant gallows, but it wasn't. She strained some ligaments, and there was an angry red rope burn the size of a Triscuit on her neck.

Naturally, she wanted to try it again. Naturally, I supported this decision. You get back on the horse that threw you; everyone knows that. Naturally, as I say, I did not want her to try it again.

Naturally, I wanted everyone to take the accident as a sign from heaven and change the plans, throw out the trick, move to Cleveland.

Naturally, I didn't say any of this; naturally, I just smiled vaguely and got the worst headache of my adult life. I did not stay to see the trick tried again; I squinted my way home and went to bed. My dreams were earshattering, appalling. The ceiling demons howled; the hot pillow hordes, the blood-damp hell-riders.

And then it was time for opening night. "You must be a proud dad," someone said in the lobby. "Must I?" I asked.

I went backstage to see Shana. We whispered in the wings. Her neck bruise was covered by makeup; she looked tightly strung but calm. I could smell that circusy blend of powder and sweat when I hugged her.

"Good luck," I said.

"I want to thank you," she said, "for being so sane through all this."

See, I'm sane. Knew it all along. We are amazing, are we not, parents and children, grace and fire, together and apart? Two small miracles in a small corner of a big stage; God save the moment. We're still alive; we must be OK.

THE WILD WOMAN OF BORNEO

Leeches do not deserve their bad reputation. They're only a few inches long, and they don't hurt, and they're relatively disease free, and you hardly miss the tiny amount of blood they drink.

People worry, but needlessly. You're in much more danger crossing the freeway.

Besides, they're inevitable in Borneo. Think jungle, think leeches. They get between your toes and under your arms, but in a nice way. They pull right off like bits of Play-Doh. No problem with leeches.

Still, I won't be going to Borneo this year. Just don't have the time. Still, my wife is going to Borneo. Has gone to Borneo. Within the last 24 hours, actually.

As I write this, she will have just landed in Jakarta. As you read this, she will be flying in a missionary plane to Long Lebusan, a mountain village in Borneo that is the home of the proud Kenyah people and about eight million leeches. The Kenyahs used to be head-hunters, but that was all a long time ago, probably.

I have mixed feelings about my wife going to Borneo for a month. I make a list of the pros and cons.

Con: Aching loneliness and a feeling of utter desperation.

Pro: Really able to keep up with the pennant races.

Some might ask: What is my wife doing in Borneo? To be candid, they have asked that. The quick answer is: She is going to defy death.

Defying death among the leeches: That is my wife's idea of a nifty vacation.

Not that I mind. Ha ha, oh my no.

So she is going to go with a group of other fun seekers on a raft down the Boh River. On the Boh River there is a gorge. Last year, a group of hotshot river rafters journeyed to Long Lebusan to give the gorge a go. An ABC film crew went with them.

Also Diana Nyad, always a bad sign. My general rule of thumb is that any event Diana Nyad covers I wouldn't want to participate in.

Anyway, the hotshots decided not to raft the gorge. We have an ABC videotape of them surveying the river from the air and saying things like "no way, baby" and "I want to keep living, thanks."

My wife is going to raft the gorge. I make a list of the pros and cons.

Con: Real good chance of death or worse happening to wife.

Pro: No leeches in gorge.

Of course, no one is going to force anyone to raft an unraftable river. If the water is high, the group will take a three-day walk through the jungle and go around the gorge. That's what the people on the ABC videotape did.

It looked fun, actually. A little mud, a few leeches, but spirits were high. My wife mentioned that to one of the organizers of the tour.

Actually, he said, that was all faked. Actually, they took helicopters around the gorge. Jungle trekking is not quite as much fun as all that. They have bacteria the size of Subarus in the jungle.

So my wife is hoping for the gorge. Once through, it's an easy float past miles of flattened, smoking rain forest destroyed by the rapacity of man. International holiday high jinks! But unique, of course.

My only regret, really, is that she's going to miss a lot of great baseball.

Editor's note: An account of this very amusing trip with many leeches and surprises can be found in Shooting the Boh *by Tracy Johnston, published by Vintage Books.*

IT'S STILL THE SAME OLD STORY

There are rules to a marriage. There is the airport rule, for instance, which holds that one member of the partnership must drive the other member of the partnership to the airport under all conditions, in all weather, no exceptions.

Then there's the footwear rule, which states neither spouse may leave more than one pair of shoes in a place other than a duly recognized closet. This does not, of course, include the shoes actually on the feet of said spouse at the time, and usually does not include footwear temporarily discarded in the bathing area.

I shall not discuss the thorny matter of bedroom slippers. This space does not wish to get involved in theological disputes.

I am also not prepared to discuss such controversial principles as You Bought It, You Clean It; You Invited Them, You Cook For Them; or If The Invitation Says 7 O'Clock, I Like To Be There At 7 O'Clock. As a wise man once remarked: There are many paths but only one road, unless the reverse is true.

But one issue that all commentators agree on is the Law Of The Oft-Told Anecdote. Both spouses enter a marriage with oft-told anecdotes; both spouses plan to continue telling them. It is the duty of the listening spouse to pay attention, not interrupt and laugh at the appropriate times.

Nothing more is necessary; nothing less is tolerable.

And now we come to the crux, as it were, of the dilemma. My spouse, the noted adventuress and tamer of wild rivers, has an anecdote that is something more than an anecdote. It is more like a narrative. It concerns her trip to Borneo and her exploration of an uncharted river on an ill-fated expedition.

The narrative contains floods, hunger, heroism, leeches, stinging insects, jungle rot, near-death experiences, waterfalls, high adventure, romance, superstitious natives, wet T-shirts and the destruction of the rain forest.

I know what you're thinking: You're thinking that the problem is that I am sick of hearing the narrative. But that is not the problem. I like hearing the narrative, and even if I didn't my social behavior is covered under the Law Of The Oft-Told Anecdote.

No, the problem is that she is tired of telling it. But people ask.

"I understand you've been to Borneo," they say. "Urgmph," says my wife. "Must have been pretty wild," the people persist. "Not really," says my wife.

"It was very wild," I say. Is that so wrong?

So then my wife tells her story. It's a darned good story, as I mentioned. I like hearing it. Then she forgets about the bees.

"Tell about the bees," I say.

"I was getting to the bees," she says.

"You always tell about the bees right before the leeches."

"Bees?" asks one of the guests.

"I don't have an order," she says.

"Maybe you do and maybe you don't, but the bees belong before the leeches. It's the jungle pest portion of the story."

"Whose story is it?"

"Bees?" says the guest again. There is a noticeable strain at the table.

I understand that I am not handling this the best way. Please don't give me that lecture about using the "I" word again. But partners over time do develop an investment in each other's anecdotes.

Suppose I told the story about the fortune teller in Jaipur and left out Jann Wenner? "Suppose I told the anecdote about the fortune teller in Jaipur and left out Jann Wenner?" I ask crushingly.

"Fortune teller?" says the guest, increasingly eager to change the subject. "That sounds interesting."

"Do tell about the fortune teller," says my wife.

"You haven't done the bees yet," I say.

"The bees are sooo boring," she says, "unlike your fabulous fortune teller story."

It only takes a little while longer for us to decide which story to tell, but by then, alas, the guest has tiptoed away, leaving only a bogus forwarding address.

AN EXPERIMENT IN HEAT EXCHANGE

This is an ordinary thing, an everyday occurrence. It happens all the time and is in no way significant or worrisome. Tracy and I have a disagreement about the heat.

I regret to say that my position is less politically correct than her position, but politics is not at the root of the discussion. Once in a great while, one or another of the panelists may mention that another of the panelists seems to be in favor of depleting the world's energy resources and leaving our children a barren inheritance of endless suffering and toil, but this is a mere side issue.

My views on children are well known, Mr. Speaker. I need not remind this body of my stirring monograph, "Let's Be Nicer to Our Kids and Let Them Pet the Farm Animals."

It is a matter of preference. It is also a matter of office location within the Greater Domestic Temperature Sphere, but essentially it is a matter of preference. I prefer more home warmth than Tracy. Our ideal thermostat settings differ by five to eight degrees on the average.

Every person has a right to his or her own opinion. I firmly believe that. See my stirring monograph, "Every Person Has a Right to His or Her Own Opinion; I Firmly Believe That."

Naturally, there have been discussions. "Oh solace of my golden years, do you not think that it is perhaps just a shade too cool in this room currently?"

Alternatively: "Oh great-hearted keeper of my heart, so you do not concur that it is just the tiniest bit stifling in here just at the moment?"

The answer to each question would be the same. "Why no, dearest-only snuggle-puppy, I do not." There would follow further discussions in which both parties would attempt, using both scientific and subjective means, to determine the Optimal Temperature Setting. These discussions would often involve the distress over declining fossil fuel reserves noted above, as well as remarks concerning incipient

arthritis in middle-aged writers, headaches caused by oxygen deple-
tion, and curious heat sinks that block the movement of warmth into
certain areas of the home.

Occasionally, in an effort to achieve greater accuracy, distances
would be paced off: the heater to the desk; the heater to the window;
the heater to the other heater. At least, that is the most logical explanation of the pacing. The exact function of the waving of the arms is
not clear.

Sometimes, additional evidence would be introduced, like "I'd like
to see you try to cook a three-course meal sometime" or "How about
that time in 1977 when we were an hour and a half late to Matthew's
party?"

But all that has changed now! We have hit upon a solution so simple in its design, so elegant in its operation, that it would seem to be a
model for problem-solving everywhere.

The solution involved abandoning the notion that there was an
Optimal Temperature Setting; indeed, the solution involved abandoning the notion that there was a solution. Rather, it involved commitment to a process.

When I walk by the thermostat, I turn it up. When she walks by,
she turns it down. Up, down, up, down. It is what it is, and then it is
something else. If it's too hot, make it cooler. If it's too cold, make it
warmer. Up, down, up, down.

The result is that the house achieves its Optimal Temperature
Setting. What we were unable to accomplish with fervent discussion,
it did with no conversation at all.

This means, I think, that our house is smarter than we are. We
hope that next year it will do our taxes—another area in which there
is no truth, only opinions and averages.

A LOVELY MORNING AT OUR HOUSE

I woke up after nine hours' sleep, an unusually long period of slumber. No real reason; maybe my body knew something I didn't. I went downstairs, brewed a pot of decaf (I'm trying to cut out caffeine; it makes me jittery) and read *The Chronicle* (that makes me nervous too, but it's more or less a requirement of continued employment).

Tracy came downstairs, poured herself a cup from the pot, and read the front section while I was buried in the box scores.

"Great, now the banks are going to fail too," she said.

"Murmph," I said.

I ate my cereal, poured another cup of coffee and strolled into my office. I had an idea for a column, actually a fine idea, a damn fine idea. I did need to make a few phone calls and check the Well (my computer conferencing system, the source of many yucks and datapoints) for some information.

So I dialed up the Well and, as I watched the scrolling letters, I made a few phone calls. I got three machines in a row, and it's pretty annoying to get a machine when you're on a deadline writing an extremely important column.

Also, on the Well someone said something about that whole intellectual property debate that was willfully stupid, so I typed a few sharp sentences in response. Then I got some electronic mail from someone asking me for a favor.

I mean, I have a column to write. Plus I can't find the information I want. Plus no one has returned my calls. Plus I called someone for a phone number. He said, "I think it's in the book." Hey, back off. I'm sailing to glory here.

So I had just started typing my column when Tracy came in and said, "I'm going to paint the ceiling."

"Which ceiling?"

"Dining room."

"Will it smell?"

"Water-based paint. Probably not."

"Fine fine fine. I'm trying to write a column here." I tried to write the column but then all the people from the machines called back.

I already had the information. Jeez. At one point I got so distracted I rearranged my file folders and scrubbed the top of the refrigerator.

Tracy came back. "Got the paint, got a couple of flats of delphiniums, three bags of mulch and new pot holders," she said.

"I am trying," I said distinctly, "to write a column."

I felt a little bad about being brisk with Tracy, so I went into the dining room, where Tracy was whipping her roller across the ceiling, and I said, "You know, it's funny how just getting a little extra sleep can make me energetic."

"Me too," she said, not stopping the roller. "It's almost, I dunno, as though the coffee had caffeine in it."

We looked at each other with wild surmise. Together, we plunged toward the garbage can. We laughed unhealthy laughs as our fingers pawed through the black banana skins and empty cat food cans. I found the bag and held it up.

"Yes!" I screamed. "It's not us! It's the coffee!"

"That's wonderful!" she said. She danced around the room like a schoolgirl, clapping and singing. "We're not crazy after all; we're not crazy after all!"

Friends, once you've decided to clean up your act, be sure to keep going. Drugs don't kill people, people kill people, but usually the people have had a mite too many chemicals beforehand.

TRUE TALES FROM THE SPORTS ZONE

So I am watching the ballgame on television and Tracy comes in and notices that I am pacing behind my chair and says, "What's happening?"

"Trevor Wilson has a no-hitter going," I said.

"Aha," she says. We've been together a long time; she has sat with me through portions of many televised baseball and football and basketball games. There are days in which she believes that what is intriguing about spectator sports is almost within reach, that a breakthrough will occur and the mysterious appeal of televised competition will suddenly become clear to her.

She knows from hundreds of overheard conversations that a "no-hitter" is a peak experience for a baseball fan. She settles herself down to watch. The first batter lifts a lazy fly ball to Kevin Mitchell.

"Well, there it goes," she says.

"What?"

"The no-hitter. There it goes."

"Oh, no. Mitchell caught the ball. It's fine."

"But the other guy hit the ball."

"Yes."

"So there goes the no-hitter," she says. And then we look at each other and realize that we have entered the sports zone again. The sports zone is not a fun place, but we do spend time there regularly.

The prognosis for communication is not good, but we try. We're a plucky little couple.

"No, see, the point of a no-hitter is that no batter hits safely for the whole game," I say.

"So in a no-hitter, they actually hit the ball?"

"They do, yes."

"Wouldn't it be even more remarkable if they didn't hit the ball?"

"But that's never been done," I say.

We look at each other again. It would be nice to report that our voices remained calm and affectionate during this entire exchange, but that is not the truth. There is tension in the sports zone. There are border guards. There are negotiations at a round table.

"I'm sure your kind of no-hitter is good, too," she says.

"Yours is definitely superior," I say. See how mature we are?

Part of it, of course, is the man-woman stuff that no one understands. Certainly there are female sports fans; certainly there are men who loathe sports. But, by and large, on the average, over the long haul, all things being equal, it is the men who watch sports and the women who don't.

Is it all cultural? Is it some weird DNA thing? Is it the territorial imperative? Is it repressed homosexuality? Does it have anything to do with world domination? Who's zooming whom?

"Maybe it's like soap operas," she said the other day. Women in general follow soap operas; men in general follow sports. Tracy doesn't follow either, but any cultural port in a storm. It is possible to argue, if you squish your mouth around funny, that sports is real people doing symbolic things and soap operas are symbolic people doing real things.

It's hard to work the Olympics into that, however. The cast of "One Life to Live" doesn't travel to Sarajevo and march around an ice rink.

Also, although Ray Knight and Nancy Lopez are actually married, we don't get to see them make out on television.

"Have fun," Tracy says, leaving. Trevor Wilson loses his no-hitter in the ninth. I go up to her office and tell her the bad news. "Too bad," she says, using the approved language of the treaty.

LOVE'S ARROW; TIME'S ARROW

Wife and self are driving back from a gracious dinner party in the fashionable bedroom community of Albany. Wife and self are driving down Marin approaching San Pablo. Seeing congestion to the left, I move to the right.

"This is a right-turn-only lane," says Tracy.

"No, it isn't," I say. "The painted arrow on the road was two pronged. I am offered an option; straight or right. I am choosing straight."

"It was not," says Tracy, calmly but definitely.

"It was so," I say, applying the gentle light of reason to the situation.

"It was not," says Tracy, introducing new evidence.

"It was so," I say, providing the clinching argument.

"One hundred dollars," says Tracy. We have entered a new area of conversation.

We have many discussions, the wife and the self. We each have varying degrees of certainty about our positions in these discussions.

When Tracy is very, very sure, she offers to bet me $100 on the matter in question.

I have lost all but one of the $100 bets. The offer to bet $100 is for me (this took some time) an indication that I should back off and reconsider. It's not the money; it's the principle of the thing. Also, it's the money.

On the other hand, I'm really sure that I saw the two-pronged arrow. I waffle between the courage of my convictions and the courage of hers.

Finally I say "done" and hang the next right.

It's 11:30 on a Saturday night, and the distinguished columnist and his authoress wife are prowling through the streets of Albany searching for the truth about the arrows. It's a trivial matter, except right at the center.

We coast slowly down Marin, two pairs of eyes scanning the asphalt.

Finally, on the roadway ahead: a two-pronged arrow. I have broken the curse of the $100 bet.

We talk about it on the way home, remembering the other $100 bets, discussing the one still pending, which has to do with whether the sun will hit the magnolia tree on April 15. It is a satisfyingly private exchange, a conversation no one else would either understand or care about.

The universe within a marriage; science fiction in everyday life.

I remember, as a younger person, looking at older couples sitting at restaurants not saying anything to each other. I can remember thinking it looked like some existential hell.

I did not understand that the universe of a marriage looks mundane and incomprehensible from the outside. You see: two ordinary people in ordinary clothes sitting at a table looking mildly at each other. We feel: a quiver of anticipation, a shock of recognition, a tremor of speculation.

Often about dumb stuff; it is the transformation of dumb stuff that is at the heart of the mystery. Arrows in the road; items on the menu; plans for the afternoon. That's what life actually is; in between the Wagner and the Cole Porter there's a lot of tuneless whistling.

The challenge is to make the whistling interesting; the challenge is to find the charm in the mundane. Doesn't always work; at least not for me. But when it does, it is (I believe) unique to each couple, a product of history so deep it is scarcely remembered.

Family jokes don't travel well; family stories have a limited audience. They are like the currency of a very tiny country, worthless in the larger world but precious in the rooms of love.

OLD KNOTS JUST GET STRONGER

There is something perfect and easy about the embrace of a long-time lover. The arms slip easily through; left up, right down, whatever; the decisions have been made although not announced.

Noses and chins and foreheads and optical appliances sort themselves out without struggle or strain; planning is not required. You mesh like well-designed gears; you fold into each other like melted butter and sweet cream; you slide like otters through calm waters.

You kiss before you know that you are kissing. The impulse; the act; nothing between.

It is said that people who have been together for a long time begin to resemble one another. It is equally possible to believe that familiarity has bred natural bumps and hollows in the body. A concave spot in the shoulder, a certain crook of the elbow, a knee automatically bent to preserve equilibrium.

Made for each other.

Literally.

This is a song about Valentine's Day, but it is not a song about young love. The confusion of young love is immediate and complete; the confusion of old love is complete and eternal. The first mystery has been solved; it is the mystery beyond (more complex, more amusing, more satisfying) that rivets the attention now.

These are embarrassing matters. New love is not embarrassing, at least not to the new lovers. So heavily involved are they in private communications—I didn't mean, I never thought, of course you, certainly you, a thousand times you—that public embarrassment fades into the wallpaper.

But eventually they swim up to consciousness again, and they become more circumspect. Compared to the volumes written about the first flush of passion, the words composed about longtime love would fill no more than a slim book.

A slim book with wide margins.

A slim book that soon finds its way to the bargain bins.

Affection informed by tolerance and patience is not a commercial emotion. Old friends and old lovers are valued privately, which is probably as it should be.

We get along; we go along; the ecstasy is implicit.

Implicit ecstasy would seem to be a paradox; the continuing experience, however, denies the apparent contradiction.

There is this moment in the longtime love affair: the moment of intellectual joy.

You have seen this person in every conceivable context. You have seen her (or him; you may freely substitute "him") at her absolute worst. Also at her best. Also during the boring moments in between.

You have seen her sleeping, unaware, innocent, slack mouthed. You have seen her awake, interested, bolt upright, un-self-conscious, eyes glittering, gathering information. You have seen her awkward and graceful; you have seen her reaping and sowing.

And just when you think you have discovered all the somethings about her, there is something else.

Valentine's Day would be a stupid holiday, were it not for that.

Were it not for the unknown at the center of the known.

Were it not for the pulse of the blood under your hands.

Were it not for the embrace of the longtime lover.

ONE SLEEPS, THE OTHER DOESN'T

Usually I wake up before she does. She has some trouble sleeping; often I see signs of her predawn ramblings in the kitchen: a still-moist cantaloupe skin, a plate with scone crumbs, apple peelings.

She never peels apples during the day; only at night. I've never asked why.

Sometimes she falls asleep with her reading light still on. Sometimes the book is right by her hand, still open. I walk around the bed and turn out the light. Usually she says something; usually I can't understand it. She never remembers later.

Sometimes, after I've turned out the light, I watch her sleep. I guess we all do, all us mated folks, although we don't talk about it much. We watch the other one sleep. So familiar and so alien, that other; so curious.

I look at her face, trying to see it for the first time, trying to remember what it looked like before I knew what it looked like. I try to compare it to the face I knew 15 years ago, see how it's aged.

There's a certain deep wonder: What does she really look like? She has merged so far into my heart that often I'm not sure I could describe her.

There are times, when I meet her at the airport, that I don't quite recognize her when she gets off the plane.

It's early as I write this; she's still upstairs asleep. Writing this makes me want to go upstairs and look at her again, but I'm afraid I'll wake her. There was a peach pit in the sink when I came down; I know she was up last night.

Sometimes, when I look at her sleeping, I wonder if she's dreaming.

I wonder if I am. I used to watch my children sleep. I think everyone does that. They're easy to sentimentalize when they're asleep; so innocent, so undemanding, so quiet. And lovely, of course—that thought is, I have been told, hard-wired into our brains; nature has made us believe that all children are lovely, so we will have another reason to protect them.

When we get older, we get uglier. Nature doesn't want us protected so much.

And the act of sleeping with someone else in the room is a gesture of trust, a gift. A sleeping child, one thinks, is a child who feels safe. You want your children to feel safe; you're happy when they sleep peacefully.

Sometimes I watch my now-adult children sleep, on trips or whatnot. I know that our relationship is far different now, but in that little moment I can enjoy the luxury of slipping back into the old ways, father watching over child.

They can decide for themselves where to live and whom to marry; I can still watch them sleep. But mostly, now, I watch her sleep. Sometimes I try to animate her face, like a cartoon. I try to remember her laughing, and then try in my mind to make that face I see on the pillow change into the laughing face I remember. I'm interested in how her muscles work, I guess;

I'm interested in how her moods animate her. Her face is generally calm when she sleeps, although there are small explosions of emotion: She frowns, sticks out her tongue, mutters, smiles.

Every time I watch her sleep is another tick of the clock, another drop in the bucket. We have come this far together, I think; we have made it through to this morning still more in love than not, still happy to be in each other's company, still paying attention.

Like sleep itself, a daily miracle.

Mondegreen Sorbet

MONDEGREENS RIPPED MY FLESH

Here at the Center for the Humane Study of Mondegreens, we've been toting up the entries and applying the latest statistical correlative methods, even using our toes, to arrive at a semi-definitive answer.

We believe that the most frequently submitted Mondegreen is still "Gladly, the cross-eyed bear" (known in the real world as that fine old hymn "Gladly The Cross I'd Bear"). A close second is "There's a bathroom on the right," a mishearing of "There's a bad moon on the rise" from the old Creedence Clearwater song "Bad Moon Rising."

Third place is still firmly held by "Excuse me while I kiss this guy," actually "Excuse me while I kiss the sky" from the Jimi Hendrix song "Purple Haze." Mr. Hendrix was himself aware that he had been Mondegreened, and would occasionally, in performance, actually kiss a guy after saying that line.

Fourth place is probably occupied by Round John Virgin, a Shakespearean figure occasionally found in "Silent Night." Also high on the charts is a Mondegreen from "Groovin'," a popular song of an earlier era. (Kids, "groovin'" was kind of like "chillin'," except the clothing fit more tightly.)

In that song, the Rascals were singing "You and me endlessly," but many people heard "You and me and Leslie," leading to speculation about the exact identity of Leslie and the popularity of multiple couplings in the music world.

For those of you who have not yet received the pamphlet (mailed free to anyone who buys me an automobile), the word Mondegreen, meaning a mishearing of a popular phrase or song lyric, was coined by the writer Sylvia Wright.

As a child, she had heard the Scottish ballad "The Bonny Earl of Murray" and had believed that one stanza went like this:

Ye Highlands and Ye Lowlands
Oh where hae you been?
They hae slay the Earl of Murray,
And Lady Mondegreen.

Poor Lady Mondegreen, thought Sylvia Wright. A tragic heroine dying with her liege; how poetic. When it turned out, some years later, that what they had actually done was slay the Earl of Murray and lay him on the green, Wright was so distraught by the sudden disappearance of her heroine that she memorialized her with a neologism.

This space has been for some years the chief publicity agent for Mondegreens. The Oxford English Dictionary has not yet seen the light, but it will, it will.

The pledge of allegiance is such a hotbed of Mondegreens that one could create a composite of submitted entries: "I pledge a lesion to the flag, of the United States of America, and to the republic for Richard Stans, one naked individual, with liver tea and just this for all."

This formulation is elderly enough to have predated "under God," which is just as well; it would be a shame to lose "one naked individual."

There are Mondegreens in familiar phrases. A friend of Adair Lara's believed for years that we live in a "doggy dog world" populated by pushy people with a "no holes barred" attitude, while a friend of

Carolyn Stone's believed that World War II was fought between the Zees and the Not Zees.

B. Young was charmed to hear that both Coke and Pepsi came in "cheerleader size." Later, he was disappointed to learn that it was actually "two litre size." Florence Jarreth was interested in the new "Jeep Parakeet," but less interested in the new "Jeep Cherokee."

James Lauder recounted the story of the pet shop clerk who told him, in all seriousness, that her parents' wealth did them no good at all because they just sat around their backyard deck in Marin and "drank themselves to Bolivia."

Geoffrey Gould's mother was convinced that if, say, you were moving a vase to a high shelf because small children were about to come over, you were moving said vase "out of arm's sway." Stephanie von Buchau always believed, correctly I should think, that "a soft dancer turneth away wrath."

But the overwhelming majority of Mondegreens come from song lyrics. Remember on the East Side and the West Side when me and Mamie O'Rourke "risked our lives in traffic"? Remember when Simon and Garfunkel sang hauntingly about how "partially saved was Mary and Tom"? Remember that touching moment in "I'm in The Mood for Love" when the singer reveals his favorite nickname for his beloved?

I'm in the mood for love,
Simply because you're near me,
Funny Butt, when you're near me. . . .

There was the Bob Dylan song with the memorable refrain: "Dead ants are my friends, they're blowin' in the wind." There was the great Crystal Gayle song "Doughnuts Make Your Brown Eyes Blue." There was the equally wonderful Maria Muldaur song "Midnight After You're Wasted."

Val Kruger heard Jose Feliciano's famous recording of "Feliz

Navidad" as "Police naughty dog," and now so will you. Barry McCarthy mentioned another popular Spanish song, "One Ton Tomato." Melissa McChesney always heard "My baby likes the Western movies" as "My baby's like a wet sock moving."

Two great Paul McCartney Mondegreens: The lines of French in "Michelle" were heard by Kathy Stawhorn's daughter as "Michelle, ma bell, Sunday monkey won't play piano song, play piano song." Several people have heard the line in "Lucy in the Sky with Diamonds" that goes "the girl with kaleidoscope eyes" as "the girl with colitis goes by."

There are many more; many more—I have envelopes stuffed with them. But our eyes grow weary and our stomachs grow hungry; we must now, in the words of the old Christmas carol, "sleep in heavenly peas."

ODD PROSE I: THE TWEEDLE RETURNS

It is of course impolite to make fun of people from other nations who create English prose. We only do it out of love, and the need to feel superior, and because we like a rollicking good time. What is humor, after all, but making other people feel bad?

Wit and wonder is where you find it; I find it in odd prose, and so does Jane J. Phillips of Berkeley, who sent along an entire brochure prepared by the Chinese National Foo-Hsing Opera Company in 1970. Of particular interest is the section entitled "Sketch of Cultivating Chinese Opera Talents":

"It is important for one to learn Chinese opera in his boyhood as a prerequisite, for it has much to do with skillful movement of both the leg and the loins. Hence, the students who are admitted to the Academy are all under the age of 12 for meeting a requirement of learning a warrior's art.

"Everyday the students at the Academy get up at dawn. After wishing their faces, they, taking advantage of the fresh air practice their voices, or sing their favorite melodies at the foot of a hill or on a lakeside near campus. Then, they begin to read their lines and to practise their tunes and their tweedle lessons and train their larynxs.

"In addition to teaching them how to sing, how to recite lines, and how to put up shows on the stage, the Academy makes out a schedule for to practice military arts and a face-to-face figting. For one thing, the first step for a beginning actor is raising his leg or bending his loins.

"That is to say, he should practice rasing his leg high up his head and should ben back gradually until he can touch his aukles, plus such actions as Swallow Dive, turning somersaults, assaulting, riding with a house-whip, walking around the stage, and To Get Armor (chi par) with them, students will lay a good foundation with a charing pose."

Sounds far too difficult; I haven't been able to touch my aukles in years. These days, I'm lucky if I can touch my house-whip.

Susan Rothbaum, also of Berkeley but apparently unaware of Jane J. Phillips (until this moment) contributed the following bewildering message, actually printed in white flocking on a bright orange promotional T-shirt:

"MESSAGE FROM HOLIDAY LAUNDRY CLUB!!!

"Nobody can say T-shirts is underwear. T shirts had been acquired citizenship. We call T, that is why we like it. Plain American tipe is a delegate T shirts. Let's change many time in a day and after excessive exercise and sweat. There is an essential feeling in American tipe T shirts. Simple print on a thin cloth. We can not part wit them after wear on definately. Printing design change one after another. These design are making by special manufacture.

"We should be add your member of wardrobe and wishes enjoy summer of this year." Ah, but if wishes were horses, would they have the citizenship of T shirts? Malcolm, fetch me my house-whip. . . .

One more: Marilyn Green of San Francisco pointed out that many of the finest examples of odd prose can be found on the backs of post cards. She submitted her favorite, from Thailand:

"Boys do not wear sombreros because they believe they can stand on the heat, but not always."

Stand on the heat, fine. But can they touch their aukles?

ODD PROSE II: THE NIGHTHORSE CONTINUES

Not to make fun but merely to have a lovely laugh, we present an entirely different universe created and maintained through the magic of odd prose, as follows:

Emily Mannion of San Francisco sent along this leaflet issued to English-speaking visitors by the Tokyo Police Department:

"At the rise of a hand from a policeman, stop rapidly. Do not pass him or otherwise disrespect him. When a passenger of the foot hoves in sight, tootle the horn trumpet at him."

Already we are in heaven, an earthly paradise featuring policemen with inflatable hands and passengers of the foot and horn trumpets that tootle, oh my, lest there be disrespect inferred or implied.

"If he still obstacles your passage, tootle him with vigor and express by word of mouth the warning 'Hi, Hi!' Beware of the wandering horse that he shall not take fright as you pass him. Go soothingly by, or stop by the roadside till he pass away. Give a big space to the festive dog that makes sport in the roadway."

The festive dog that makes sport in the roadway. Has this concept ever been more charmingly expressed?

Finally, "Go soothingly on the grease mud, as there lurks the skid demon. Press the brake of the foot as you roll around the corners to save the collapse and tie up."

We have met the skid demon and he is ours.

In the toy department, we have the "Non-Toxic Non-Edible Magic Chameleon's Tongue—Wild Animated Tongue Will Shock You Greatly!"

What is it about this tongue? "The product has stickiness, it can be stretched like soft rubber and will stick things like stick-fast glue. It is a game to play with sticking things from far away."

Some fun, this sticking things from far away. But there are cautions: "Do not throw toward head or face of person. Do not throw toward or put near the fire place. Though not toxic, it is forbidden to eat. Do not overstretch the tongue of the Chameleon, otherwise, it will go off."

Not your cup of tea? How about the Super Skiing Penguins? "Dear Customer: As a cleanly creature, penguins may get ill and refuse to ski when constant operations cause dust. Take care of your cute friends as below and you would share the incredible joy of their race . . . Penguins will become crippled when forced to ski on the floor."

As who would not?

Finally, we have this marvelous brief biography of the composer Vincenzo Bellini from the liner notes of a record album produced in Italy:

"Bellini was born in Catane in 1801. Old of 18, he is admeted to the College of St-Sebastien in Naples. His first Oper 'Adelson e Salvini' written in 1825 is the beginning of his career. Chopin and Wagner admired him. We see badly that master of the Bel Canto writting a concerto for hautboy and here is a work with a big beauty. Through these melodies and his joice to life, this work written by a young men of 20 years old, takes immediately the adhesion."

A work with a big beauty taking the adhesion. One is almost embarrassed to watch. You don't suppose that joice is . . . James?

ODD PROSE III: COFFEE AND BALLS

I know I should be out performing works of benefit to all mankind, but I just have to stay indoors reading my ever-growing treasure trove of strange English, some of it in translation, some of it not.

Today's first entry was sent by Francesca Busch of Berkeley. It is the instruction leaflet from a Japanese toy called Magic-Balls. I quote because I must:

"Magic-Balls are production, an originative playing. These funny balls can be piled up to combine into a variety of towers, pyramids, cubes, buildings, equipment, human figures or fascinating models. The piling-up and combination hold definitive stability because the balls are magnet-possessed. The playing of these balls can lead the player to indefinite development of his fancy and originality."

Magnet-possessed. You bet. Been there; done that.

"In addition, the playing is an amusement indeed. For instance, by combining these interesting Magic-Balls one can carry out such plays as: ball collision by transcending different metallic obstacles, dicing in any way that the number may be selected, and successful shooting at an object on a round metal or marble plate placed on the floor. The results of these plays are highly surprising and praisable."

Magic-Balls. Pick some up at your metallic obstacle outlet today.

What else? Ann Whipple of San Francisco sent me a brochure for the EMC Ice Mud Making Machine ("High precision, rich parts & fittings available everywhere at inexpensive"), but half the joy is in the diagram, which I can't reproduce.

Ice Mud is apparently the substance found in sno-cones. It is a useful and vivid term, and I urge its general adoption.

Richard Grant of San Francisco sent me the package from Special Blue Mountain Blend Coffee, upon which are printed the following cautionary words:

"World Coffee leads the coffee of the world. World Coffee is a superior blend of strictly selected beans on persistent pursuit of dainty.

"To keep permanently these best quality of world coffee, the air has been extracted and for that reason appears compact, but when you open the packing, the product will recover the aspect of perfect ground coffee."

In my personal pursuit of dainty, I always try to keep an Ice Mud Maker nearby and, of course, a complete set of Magic-Balls. The results are surprising and praisable.

Finally, Tim Miller of Stockton reminded me that art criticism is a rich mine for nuggets of pure bewildering joy. He enclosed an article from a 1978 issue of *Art Forum* by one Joseph Masheck. I emphasize that this is not a translation. Here is the first paragraph:

"Paintings involved with cruciformality can raise, and then transcend, the question of their being sculptural. Ultimately they affirm their affinities with painting by being shaped, shape-displacing objects only to the same extent that other paintings are. Painting reflects concern back from an only negligibly space-displacing esthetic territory into the observers' world, whereas sculpture generally already substantially inhabits the space to which it refers or alludes."

In other words, a sculpture is three dimensional and a painting ain't, even if it's a painting of a cross.

There's a hot premise.

AT LONG LAST: A NEW GAME

Let us for instance take the topic "rumors." Wasn't it Fred Allen who said: "No matter what kills you, it's the rumors that'll pick your bones clean?"

Well, no it wasn't. It was Michael J. Hogan of Santa Rosa who said that. Michael J. Hogan is (or claims to be) the inventor of a new game, a good game, a game that we as columnist and reader can play together. The name of the game is "Fake Quotes." Oh, no it's not. That's what Hogan calls it, but he is being too modest.

The name of the game is "Hoganisms."

The idea is to come up with a topic and then ask everybody to make up quotes in the manner of various frequently quoted people. Fred Allen is the example above; Hogan thoughtfully provides many more fictitious quotations on the same subject:

"Eighty percent of rumors are wrong. Most reliable damn source we've got."—Samuel Clemens.

"Save your communiques. Tell me the rumors."—Calvin Coolidge.

"Rumors are apprentice myths."—Joseph Campbell.

"You writers make up rumors when you can't think of any." —Yogi Berra.

"We keep hearing the hungry are homeless, the homeless are hungry, and the elderly are aging. We can't change established policies just because of rumors."—Dan Quayle.

"For journalism, reports are enough. For literature, you need rumors."—E. B. White.

"She felt the rough skin of his rugged yet tender hands and her bosom swelled in her bodice like a rumored sunrise." —Judith Krantz.

The last one isn't really about rumors and is, therefore, cheating, but I do try to use cheap tricks to boost readership whenever possible.

So here's the deal. This space hereby invites its beloved readers to submit fake quotes, together with their bogus authors, on any or all of these three topics: "Fame," "Marriage" and/or "Vegetables."

No real quotations, please. No fair picking something from Oscar Wilde and putting Truman Capote's name on it, either. Genuine 100 percent fake, please; even a scintilla of truth will be cause for disqualification.

This space will award a Grand Prize in each of the three categories. The Grand Prize consists of the sentence "(Your name here) wins the Grand Prize" published in the largest newspaper in Northern California.

This space will also publish other entries of high quality. Enter as many times as you like; neatness does not count although legibility is a must. Contest closes when I get enough entries.

****

Yes, the entries came flooding in. Sacks of wit; stacks of repartee. It renewed my confidence in the readers of this fine space — confidence that had never flagged, of course, despite that difficult time we went through over the divisive Pele Dancing* thing.

Naturally, being active readers with monkey minds, you chose to do more than merely submit fake quotations attributed to real people on the topics of marriage, fame or vegetables. You chose, for instance, to suggest changes in the name of the game itself.

Hogan's Slogans? Hogan's Hoax Quotes? Quotoids? Faux Mots? Each of them better than "Hoganisms," no doubt. There's probably a better name for poker than "poker," too—Big Ace, maybe—but poker is poker and Hoganisms are Hoganisms and we can't change horses in midstream, as Benjamin Franklin or Mark Twain or Daniel Webster once remarked.

There was some misunderstanding as to the exact nature of the contest. Some sought, not verisimilitude or aphoristic balance, but mere irony. "Fidelity is important in marriage"—John Kennedy; that sort of thing.

*Don't ask.

Others, I fear, let private fantasies run away with them: "Fame is to turnips as the priesthood is to marriage."—Pope John Paul II; intriguing, certainly, but hard to justify within the parameters of the contest.

There was some repetition. It seemed that many readers had heard that George Bush hated broccoli; they were also aware that Adolf Hitler was a vegetarian. This conjunction led to whimsical combinations that were not, perhaps, entirely patriotic.

Some people veered utterly from the rules in the hopes that I would find the results so amusing that I would print them anyway, regardless of their relevance. Only Paul Wagner of Napa succeeded:

"Gettysburg, Pa. My dear Joseph, the rumors are flying through this town like dry leaves before the wind. Each day, each breath of air, brings a new story more dreadful than the last. What is lost, what is won? We shall never know until this terrible enterprise is done and our countries and our families are whole again. Is this to be our heritage? I cannot bear to think it. I write you these words full knowing that they will become nothing more than the narration to a public television documentary."

The vegetable category received the fewest entries of merit. We will deal with those today, handing out the coveted Grand Prize (Vegetable Division); tomorrow we'll plunge into Marriage and Fame.

It is of course not fair that Michael J. Hogan of Santa Rosa should win the game he invented, but he did submit some lovable entries: "The most frightening thing in the world? Beets."—Vincent Price. "Don't talk to me about plant life. I interview baseball players for a living."—C.W. Nevius. "Trees are easy. The challenge is to see the Divine Plan in dandelions."—Jon Carroll.

There's more. "You're not so smart. I've eaten lettuce with better heads than yours."—Groucho Marx (James Hurd).

"Vegetables are what if you didn't eat, you wouldn't be as healthy as."—Gracie Allen (Dan C. Putnam of Calistoga).

"I dislike vegetables for the same reason that I dislike most men - they're not rich enough"—Marla Maples (Carla Mertins of Livermore)

All worthy, certainly. But the Grand Prize winner in the Vegetable Division is Michael Rice of Sacramento for his immortal "Vegetables aren't my meat and potatoes."—Yogi Berra.

****

Yesterday, as readers with functioning synapses will recall, we awarded the coveted Grand Prize in the Vegetable Division; today we tackle the rather more complex Fame and Marriage categories. Below are some examples provided by readers on the subject of Fame:

"You know as well as I, Watson, that fame is often the precursor of tragedy."—Arthur Conan Doyle (Mike Embley of Rohnert Park).

"You want fame, darling? Do something famous."—Tallulah Bankhead (Scott Beach).

"You can't wear fame, but it accessorizes well."— Vidal Sassoon (Susan Williams of Concord).

"A famous person is someone you've heard of who has never heard of you."—Johnny Carson (Bob Laurence of Stockton).

"My cabinet is full of famous men. Ask any of them."—Abraham Lincoln (Paul Kay of Berkeley).

"Fame? Pah! To drag myself through public offal like so much prosperous jelly?"—Ludwig Wittgenstein (Kristen Baumgardner, who said that line came to her in a dream).

"You can't eat fame but you sure can live fine off it."—Mark Twain (Alan Nichols of San Francisco).

"Whoever said fame is fleeting has never seen 'Hollywood Squares.'"—Thurgood Marshall (J. Patrick Boushell). OK, I don't get the Thurgood Marshall part either, but the line is too lovely to lose.

"The country's most famous dentist was Doc Holliday and he carried a gun. That should tell you something."—Jay Leno (Dennis Reichard of San Francisco).

"Fame: a long period of hoping for it and a long period of hiding from it, separated by two or three nights of fun."—Rob Lowe (Michael

J. Hogan himself, for whom the game is named).

"Men want fame for better women; women want fame to better men."—Norman Mailer (Frank Puccio).

And the absolute Grand Prize winner in the Fame Division:

Fame's a worthless bauble,
A husk without a core,
A glittering chunk of fool's gold
I'd give my eye teeth for.
—Dorothy Parker (John Kelley of Berkeley).

And now, Marriage. "Marriage provides guilt, just as an audience does applause. It's the thing that makes the performance worthwhile."—Oscar Wilde (Rick Stivers of Hayward).

"Why, if we were to marry, we would no longer correspond."— Jane Austen (Will Walker of San Francisco).

"I'm not against marriage. It's fidelity I find difficult, and I do think that's important in marriage."—Warren Beatty (Ellen Hayes of Los Osos).

"It starts with passion and leads to laundry."—Lillian Hellman (Michael J. Hogan, again).

"God invented sex; priests invented marriage."—Voltaire (Bruce Tyler of Sacramento).

The Grand Prize winner in the popular Marriage Division is "It takes a very good husband to be better than no husband at all."—Mae West (Donna Davis of Half Moon Bay).

Thanks to all who participated. Next year, perhaps another contest. Please, no more Hoganisms until you hear the magic twanger.

SPECIALIST IN WOMEN AND OTHER DISEASES

One of the 84 known subcategories of humor is the commercial sign written in a language not native to the country in which the sign is found. A recent list of prime examples has been making its way through the computer networks; allegedly, its origin is an Air France memo.

It's hard to know how real these signs are. Almost certainly, many have been shortened or rephrased to make them funnier; a few may be outright inventions. Nevertheless, as any traveler knows, this art form does exist.

Nor, of course, are English speakers innocent of provoking the same merriment in other countries. One only has to remember the multimillion-dollar campaign that introduced Coca Cola to China a few years ago. Its proud slogan, emblazoned everywhere, trumpeted: "Bite the wax tadpole."

Thus and herewith:

From a Tokyo Hotel: "Is forbidden to steal hotel towels please. If you are not a person to do such a thing is please not to read notis."

In a Bucharest hotel lobby: "The lift is being fixed for the next day. During that time we regret that you will be unbearable."

In a Yugoslavian hotel: "The flattening of underwear with pleasure is the job of the chambermaid."

On the menu of a Swiss restaurant: "Our wines leave you nothing to hope for."

In an advertisement by a Hong Kong dentist: "Teeth extracted by the latest Methodists."

In a Belgrade hotel elevator: "To move the cabin, push button for wishing floor. If the cabin should enter more persons, each one should press a number of wising floor. Driving is then going alphabetically by national order."

In a Rhodes tailor shop: "Order your summers suit. Because is big rush we will execute customers in strict rotation." In an Austrian hotel catering to skiers: "Not to perambulate the corridors during the hours of repose in the boots of ascension."

In a Bangkok temple: "It is forbidden to enter a woman even a foreigner if dressed as a man."

In a Norwegian cocktail lounge: "Ladies are requested not to have children at the bar."

In a Copenhagen airline office: "We take your bags and send them in all directions." In an Acapulco hotel: "The manager has personally passed all the water served here."

On the menu of a Polish hotel: "Salad a firm's own make; limpid red better soup with cheesy dumplings in the form of a finger; roasted duck let loose; beef rashers beaten up in the country people's fashion."

In a Zurich hotel: "Because of the impropriety of entertaining guests of the opposite sex in the bedroom, it is suggested that the lobby be used for that purpose."

A sign posted in a German park: "It is strictly forbidden on our black forest camping site that people of different sex, for instance, men and women, live together in one tent unless they are married with each other for that purpose."

On the door of a Moscow hotel room: "If this is your first visit to the USSR, you are welcome to it."

In a Macao store: "Sorry! Midgets will always be available tomorrow!"

The headline of this column, by the way, is a sign outside a doctor's office in Rome.

HOW TO TOK PISIN ISSI

We were driving in from the airport at Port Moresby, Papua New Guinea, burdened with excess baggage and culture shock, when I saw the sign. It was black on yellow, over the entrance of what appeared to be a dry-goods emporium. It said "Stret Pasin Stoa."

"What's that?" I asked Jack, who had been in Moresby for six months and was presumably clued in to cultural arcana.

"It's really a chain," he said unhelpfully.

"Interesting," I said. "But what does the sign mean?"

"It's Pidgin," he said. "It's easier if you pronounce it. Stret Pasin Stoa; straight person's store. A store, in other words, run by honest fellows. Straight carries no implication of sexual orientation." "Tell me more," I said dreamily; there was something about the sound and spelling of Pidgin that entranced me. It was like Esperanto created by someone with a sense of humor.

That night, Jack gave me the definitive work on the subject, *The Jacaranda Dictionary and Grammar of Melanesian Pidgin*, plus *Tok Pisin* ("Talk Pidgin"), which is sort of the stripped down version for hurried travelers.

Pidgin is not broken English, or a dialect of English, or baby talk. It's a real language, with its own grammar, syntax and spelling. It is related to English in the same way that Italian is related to Latin.

Pidgin is a trade language, developed to facilitate communication between people of different language groups. "Pidgin" is a corruption of the Chinese pronunciation of "business."

There are several other notable "business" languages, including Afrikaans (South Africa), Swahili (Kenya) and Bahasa (Indonesia). The Melanesian variety, which is the lingua franca of Papua New Guinea, is called Pidgin, or Pisin.

To the untutored ear, three words seem to dominate spoken Pidgin: "tok," "long" and "pela." The first of these, "tok," can mean talk or word or even complaint.

The most important compound of "tok" is "wantok." Your "wantok" (one talk) is your friend, a member of the same clan, a person to whom you have a significant obligation. The wantok is the primary social bond. Expats (short for expatriates, that is, people of the Caucasian persuasion) even use it as a verb: "I've been wantoked" means "I hired all these people not knowing they were in the same clan and I fired one of them and they all left simultaneously."

Similarly, "tokbek" (talk back) is an answer, "tok insait" (talk inside) is one's conscience and "tok ples" (talk place) is one's native language.

The word "long" is far more confusing. As a preposition, it can mean in, on, at, to, from, about, with or by. Thus, "Mi sori long yu" means "I feel sorry for you," and "go long gaden" means "to go to the garden."

Equally versatile is "bilong," which generally denotes the possessive but has a variety of other meanings. My two favorite examples are "Bia Bilong Yumi" (the beer that belongs to you and me), the slogan of South Pacific Beer, brewed in Moresby; and "Nambawan pikinini bilong Quin" (the Queen's number one child), referring to Prince Charles.

("Pikinini"—pickaninny—though considered a racist locution over here, is perfectly acceptable in Pidgin. It derives from the Portuguese "pequeninho," meaning little.)

"Pela" (fellow) is a suffix used in all sorts of ways. "Bikpela" is big, "gutpela" is good, "nupela" is new. Numbers up to 12 also use pela: "wanpela, tupela. . . ."

"Pela" also figures in some mind-boggling compound pronouns, including "yumitupela" (the two of us) and "yutripela" (the three of you). Knowing that, translate the following sentence: "Yesus, Maria na Yosef, tripela i stap long tempel."

Bikpela Jon i rait long nuispepa bilong San Francisco long tok ples, yes? Bikpela Jon i rait: "Jesus, Mary and Joseph were at the temple."

My Opinions

DYNAMIC DECENCY MAKES A COMEBACK

From a full-page advertisement placed by *Good Housekeeping* magazine in several national newspapers: "The Decency Decade Begins Today. Good Housekeeping Is Its Voice. Welcome to the Decency Decade, the years when the good guys finally win. We at Good Housekeeping have seen the '90s—with the help of a new study for Good Housekeeping by marketing futurist Faith Popcorn of BrainReserve—and we like what we've seen. . . ."

This is the new advertising, the advertising that tells you what the old advertising could not tell you. This advertising tells you about a magazine that really really believes that you're not a failure.

It was the world's fault. The world hated decent people like you.

But now the world doesn't. Now the good guys win. Good guys like you, with good magazines.

This is a new decade, a decent decade. We have all new people and all new institutions and everything will change right away. Why? A magazine named *Good Housekeeping* and a woman named Faith Popcorn. That's today's decency.

Remember Herman Kahn? Forget Herman Kahn. Faith Popcorn. Does she make it up as she goes along? Of course not. This is the new decency, the decency that looks you in the eye and says: Buy this magazine.

Today you can embrace an old woman in the street. Today you can shed a tear for a lonely child. Today you can work hard and believe in the future. Last month you couldn't do that. Last month the bad guys were winning. All that has changed.

More from the advertisement: "It will be a very good decade for consumers. The 'health hype' and phony claims will soon be over, as skeptical, caring New Traditionalists ignore the sizzle and demand the steak. They will judge products not only for their quality, but also for the integrity and ethical behavior of their manufacturer. They will look for what is real, what is honest, what is quality, what is valued, what is important."

This is the new advertising, the advertising that admits that it lied to you. For 50 years, we were really *Bad Housekeeping*. We went with the health hype; we went with the phony claims.

That was the Old Tradition, the Tradition of the bad guys.

But you are different; you are decent. We can no longer sell you sizzle without steak, sizzle without nutritive value. You demand better, you demand tradition, you demand "quality" used as an adjective.

It's the New Syntax.

This is a new decade; this is the new decade of the New Slogan.

This is the New Slogan: "America Is Looking for Something to Believe In." It's the slogan of the steak, not the sizzle. It's the slogan of ethical manufacturing. It's the slogan of Faith Popcorn. It's the slogan of the New Traditionalist Feminist. Not the Old Feminist, the butch one without the sense of humor. No, the New Traditionalist Feminist wears sensible yet attractive clothing. She manufactures ethically. She believes in a magazine, a magazine of Housekeeping.

Fine Housekeeping. Skeptical, Caring Housekeeping. Good Housekeeping. No dust bunnies, no steakless sizzle.

The New Traditionalists of the Decency Decade are looking for something to believe in. They have chosen *Good Housekeeping* magazine.

This is the hype without the health, the phony without the claim, the faith without the popcorn. *January, 1990*

126

GREAT BIG HATS AND LOTS OF CREAM

Some people with limited attention spans have a little difficulty with the terms "private sector" and "public sector." Sometimes, when a politician says, "this is a private-sector problem," it's hard to know exactly what he means.

Fortunately, Secretary of the Interior Donald Hodel of our very own Reagan administration has provided us with a perfect example, almost a mnemonic device, that enables us to make this distinction.

OK, so the ozone layer is being destroyed. We know this. There's this hole above Antarctica and everything. If the ozone layer deteriorates, many more of us will get skin cancer.

And we think we know why the ozone layer is being destroyed; it's those funny chemicals from the air conditioners. The evidence is pretty clear on this point, actually.

So: What would be the "public-sector" solution to this problem of all of us getting skin cancer in the next 25 years? It would be an immediate ban on the devices that produce the chemicals that break up the layer, perhaps supplemented with some government help in developing new types of air conditioners so we don't have to drip all over each other on hot days.

But this administration is dedicated to "private-sector" solutions. What is the private-sector solution to the ozone layer problem?

Big hats, sunglasses and lots of skin cream.

Let me say that to you again, friends, so that you can hear the message and understand it. You are at risk of dying of skin cancer, and an authorized, high-ranking official of your government has proposed that you solve the difficulty with (all together now) big hats, sunglasses and lots of skin cream.

Why stop there? Let's expand the notion of private-sector initiative to other areas of life. What, for instance, would be the private-sector solution to air pollution?

How about: filters surgically implanted in your respiratory tract?

Some of us older folks might have difficulty with that, but within a generation we could do it routinely at birth.

Acid rain? How about great, big overcoats for all the trees in Canada? Hell of a growth industry. Private-sector thinking at its most creative.

If that doesn't work, how about bark cream?

"Private sector" is just a matter of an individual taking responsibility for his or her own life. If, for instance, you were run over by a gigantic truck careening through an intersection where there should have been a stop sign, the "public-sector" approach would be to criticize, fine and/or otherwise humiliate the highway department or relevant municipal officials.

The private-sector approach (much cheaper; much easier) is homier, almost motherly: You knew it was dangerous; you shouldn't have been there in the first place.

Or suppose you've been denied employment because you are a woman. Public sector: Outlaw discrimination on the basis of gender. Private sector: Sex-change operations are cheaper than ever.

You cannot change your race through medical techniques. This administration understands that. So suppose you have been (say) prevented from renting the apartment of your choice because you're black. What is the private-sector solution? You got it: Big hat, sunglasses, lots of skin cream. *June, 1987*

ON SETTING A GOOD EXAMPLE

It was a terrible thing. A terrible thing. Felix Mitchell, boss of the '69 Mob, convicted racketeer, heroin dealer and gangster, received a hero's funeral last week in Oakland. A bronze coffin, a horse-drawn carriage, a procession of luxury automobiles, a parade route lined with spectators—nothing but the best for Felix.

It was reported that Felix Mitchell had been a generous man in his East Oakland neighborhood. He gave away cash and ice cream and basketballs to neighborhood kids; he provided protection for certain favored residents.

Naturally, right-thinking people were appalled at the inherent glamour of the Mitchell funeral. It was the glorification of evil, they said. As of course it was.

Right-thinking people refused to allow their children to view the funeral. It might give them the wrong idea.

On the other hand, few if any of the dissenters had spent much time in East Oakland giving away basketballs and $20 bills. The Felix Mitchell funeral was deplorable, but it was not inexplicable.

You dance with the guy who brought you to the party. In East Oakland (and in East Berkeley, and in West Marin), that's one of the basic tenets of morality.

Loyalty trumps the law; always has, always will.

The same day as the Mitchell funeral, another story broke in the Bay Area. Wilkes Bashford, the clothing magnate who pleaded *nolo contendere* to bilking the city of San Francisco out of something close to one million dollars, finally received the first part of his harsh sentence.

("Nolo contendere" is a cute little legal loophole mostly utilized by the powerful. It means that the defendant declines to contest the charges while not admitting that any wrongdoing took place. It is the legal equivalent of the Betty Ford clinic.)

Some of Bashford's powerful friends would have liked to get him off the hook entirely; they couldn't quite get the whole thing dismissed, although they came close. The kids who got money from Felix Mitchell did not, by contrast, have a lot of juice downtown.

Bashford was sentenced to putting on a charity fashion show in conjunction with the opening of his new store. The time that Bashford spends on the show will be deducted from his 1200 hours of community service, and all proceeds from the show will go to youth and criminal justice programs in San Francisco.

Less reasonable expenses. Of course.

Such a deal. Of course, it might be argued that, had Wilkes paid his full rent each and every month, that million bucks might have been sitting in city accounts drawing interest and/or going to support worthy social programs. But water under the bridge, right?

It might also be argued that since charity openings are a regular feature of San Francisco society, sentencing Wilkes to put on a worthy-cause fashion show is a little like sentencing Charlotte Mailliard to organize the Black & White Ball.

Plus, of course, Bashford gets a million dollars worth of free publicity for his new store. Oh please, Mr. Judge, don't throw me in dat briar patch.

Felix Mitchell was at least sentenced to life without possibility of parole in a Kansas prison. There he died, painfully and alone, at age 32. Wilkes Bashford was sentenced to live in his own home, in his own town, where he will be forced to throw lavish parties.

Should be a gala event, but I don't think I'll let my kids attend. They might get the wrong idea. *September, 1986*

THAT'S THE WAY THE MISSILE FIZZLES

So we have these Trident 2 missiles fall down go boom. Up they come out of the water, kablooey they go immediately thereafter and the constituent elements fall into the ocean. A lovely bit of performance art, but not exactly what the Navy was looking for.

And why, you may well ask, did this happen? Because the scientists in charge failed to take into account the effects of water turbulence on the missile.

Dig it. We've got a major, much-beloved weapons system that involves firing a missile through water, and the thing blows up because no one remembered about the water. Hello?

It's not just we civilians who are bewildered. Matthew Bunn, a senior research analyst with the Arms Control Association, a private research group, remarked, "They knew how big the missile was and they knew what the basic properties of water were and somebody probably should have seen that the one would have caused problems with the other."

I believe that to be a fair summation of the situation.

Now, I'm enough of an unrecovered hippie to experience a small frisson of excitement when the military messes up. Maybe, I think to myself for the 100th time, someone will finally get the idea and stop writing blank checks to these whimbrains.

But we're actually all on the same side, and this unending series of lamebrain, nonfunctioning weapons is disturbing. At least in the bad old days, the military knew how to wage war; at least their bullets hit the right targets.

So what's going on? Here's my theory: Start with the notion that most people are trying to do the right thing. Most people want to be honorable and decent; most people want to show up and tell the truth. Experience indicates that this is true. Most people, most of the time, try to do their best.

But the weapons procurement business tilts the other way.

Between bureaucratic face-saving, patriotic posturing and plain old corruption, it's just not fun to work for the government. So what happens? People don't.

Most people don't want to be on a gravy train; most people don't want to live within the genteel terror of an incompetent organization. So the best people get out, or they never get in.

It's all very quiet, all very road-not-taken, but you wake up one day and you've got a submarine-launched missile that doesn't work in the water.

A lot of people are getting out of the business of thing-making altogether, because many of the neatest things can only be made with government support, and who needs that grief?

So the only people who work for the government, the only people willing to fill out the forms and kiss the butts and look the other way, are the folks who don't care all that much about the quality of the finished product. There are some areas of research (computer games, for instance) that don't need government money and still offer a relatively large amount of freedom; ingenuity and care are still very much alive and well there.

Look at it this way: The people who design computer games would definitely have remembered about the water. *August, 1989*

WEIRD FLAG CULT HITS LOCAL NATION

Remember that the American synonym for "patriotic demagoguery" is "flag waving." Remember that political villains attempting to distract attention from their misdeeds are said to be "hiding behind the flag." What is happening just now is neither new nor surprising; it's a tradition as old as the republic.

Pete Wilson, who is rapidly becoming a danger to himself and others, is proposing a constitutional amendment to ban flag burning. There's an important campaign, huh? Something you'll want to donate a lot of time and money to: fabric abuse prevention.

Since the Congress can't agree on anything, not even where to find enough honest politicians to form a leadership structure, it has decided to chuck it all and wallow in rhetoric. The flag, the flag; let's see how many buttons we can push about the flag.

The most sure-fire of these arguments against the Supreme Court decision granting constitutional protection to citizens who burn flags was that brave young men had died for that flag and that therefore, etcetera and so forth.

I hope they didn't die for a flag. I hope they died for the republic for which it stands, one nation, indivisible. I hope they died for whatever they found most valuable in this country and its system of government—economic opportunity, perhaps, or individual freedoms, or free elections, or an uncorrupt judiciary.

A flag is a symbol of those things, and people who died for those things honor both themselves and us. But a symbol is not the same as the thing itself. A symbol is just an artistic version of an idea, and an idea may be disputed. It's the American way.

The people who burn flags are citizens, too, and they are taking some risks by their actions. They are risking social ostracism, for instance; in some cases they are risking physical violence. It is a brave thing to burn a flag when you are surrounded by people who disagree with the act.

Additionally, they are almost certainly doing damage to their cause.

Burning a flag is not a particularly good way to get recruits. If you could raise campaign funds by burning a flag, members of Congress would already be doing it.

So it is an act of passion, not cynicism. It springs from a belief that the flag symbolizes the less wonderful aspects of America: economic exploitation, for instance, or environmental insensitivity, or even corruption of the legislative branch.

It is the expression of an idea, therefore it is a form of speech. If it weren't a form of speech, no one would be opposed to it. It is the content of the speech that is at issue, and the Constitution is rather clear about regulating the content of speech. "Congress shall make no law . . ." is what it says.

Freedom of speech is a tough one, because sooner or later everybody's ox gets gored. My ox was a bleeding mass of fibrous tissue after eight years of Ronald Reagan exercising his freedom of speech, but that's the breaks.

Freedom of speech forces us to acknowledge one another, which eventually forces us into civilized discourse, which forces us into negotiation, which forces us into stability. But, hey: It's not just a good idea. It's the law. *June, 1989*

THE ART THING IS GETTING OUT OF HAND

Let us ask the most basic question: Why should the American public use its hard-earned dollars to pay an artist to take a photograph of a crucifix totally immersed in his own urine? This is not how Van Gogh started. For one thing, you have to be told that it's urine in the glass, which means that the image does not stand alone; it has to come with a prerecorded announcement.

Maybe it's a trend: Talky Art. Sort of like Chatty Cathy. Just pull a string and a strange android voice provides the relevant information.

In this case, it would be sort of like Chatty Cathy crossed with Baby Wets-A-Lot. It's not conceptual; it's just awkward.

Now, I'm sure it's a meaningful statement about the failure of Catholicism in today's modern world (unless the artist intends it as a depiction of the success of Catholicism in today's modern world), but it's not exactly a statement that's going to set a lot of taxpayers thinking about religion in American life.

You have to be pretty cosmopolitan to get beyond the urine part; that's just true.

If payroll taxes were itemized by the government and listed on your salary check stub—"Look, dear, I contributed $50 to the B-2 bomber and three cents to this urine-soaked cross deal"—I suspect there would be even more unhappiness than there currently is.

So come on. Should American taxpayers actually fork over bucks for bad art that is additionally offensive to a large segment of the populace? Well, of course they should.

We want to support art because art enriches us. If you want to argue that government should get out of the art business altogether, that's another quarrel. The congresshumans who want to prohibit certain kinds of art definitely want government in the art business, in order to better suppress the kind of art they don't like.

How does art enrich us? We don't know. Art is organized mystery. We can't order it up like a cheeseburger. Today, please, we'd like

$100,000 worth of the dignity of the horny-handed son of toil, with perhaps a few K of reflections on mortality for contrast.

Doesn't play. We know more or less how a plane flies, so we know what should go into it to make it fly better. Therefore, the government can usefully provide specifications to plane manufacturers.

But we don't know what makes art work. We don't know where it comes from; we don't really know why some people can do it and some people can't. Humility is really the only sane reaction in the face of great art, which is why politicians distrust it so much.

So politicizing the art process just results in bad art. Sentimental and hypocritical art numbs the senses; it makes us less than human.

Art right now is filled with taboo subjects because society is filled with taboo subjects. They talk about anal intercourse on Donahue now; interchangeable atheists and communists make late-night radio marginally more interesting.

A lot of it is nonsense, of course; 90 percent of everything is crap, as someone once remarked. But there is beauty and insight as well, and taxpayers (who are just citizens with money) have a stake in encouraging that beauty. Art is like an emotions demo; it shows us where we feel.

And the artist is a sort of scout for society; he goes ahead and sees what we cannot yet see for ourselves. We should not shoot our scouts if we don't like what they see; we are going to be living in their present soon enough.   *August, 1989*

THE REVISED STANDARD VERSION

"I did, in fact, testify truthfully, honestly, and straightforwardly to the best of my recollection on all questions that were asked of me," said William Bradford Reynolds, President Reagan's nominee for associate attorney general. ". . . My recollection with regard to the Louisiana meeting has failed me, and I have confused that with one of the other redistricting meetings."
—News item

Testimony of Jonathan Richard Carroll, President Reagan's nominee for the post of deputy acting values czar (Western division):

Senators, since our last meeting, certain facts have come to my attention that shed new light on certain incidents described (incorrectly, as it turns out) by me in earlier testimony before this distinguished body.

Despite my ceaseless dedication to complete candor, I seem to have misinterpreted or misrepresented certain relevant incidents and events.

I would now like to set the record straight.

First, with regard to the Louisiana meeting. Photographs shown to me (and distributed to the media) make it obvious that none of the public officials in question were wearing ball gowns over lavender leotards.

Also, contrary to my earlier testimony, no one, during the course of that meeting, sang all 12 verses of "Desolation Row" by Robert Dylan while brandishing a sharpened pencil. Nor was industrial flooring hurled at representatives of the International Red Cross.

In addition, the distinguished junior senator from Arkansas did not, as I earlier had stated, eat an entire dinette set. My memory failed me on that. It was a sincere error.

I turn now to the Rhode Island meeting. I fear that, in earlier testimony, I confused that conference with a made-for-TV movie I had seen in my motel room the night before.

Suffice it to say, the counsel for the 11 deaf schoolchildren involved in the case did not attempt to seduce a Jesuit priest who had been active in the Baltimore soup kitchen movement. Nor did a plastique bomb destroy the conference room just before noon.

Contrary to my earlier testimony, I was not killed during the terrorist attack. In fact, there was no terrorist attack, although the phones did cease to work for a short time just before the morning coffee break.

My earlier statement to this committee, that I would "freeze in hell" before supporting affirmative action lawsuits, has been widely misinterpreted. Hell is traditionally a place of fire and burning; therefore, "freezing in hell" would be an essentially positive experience, engendering joyful emotions similar to those that I would feel if I were lucky enough to argue in favor of affirmative action.

With regard to my instructions from the President: Mr. Reagan at no time said to me "Seen one civil right, seen 'em all." What he actually said was: "I have seen civil rights, and I stand tall."

Mr. Chairman, this administration is absolutely in favor of civil rights. Some might disagree about methodology, but none can quarrel with our basic commitment.

As deputy acting values czar, I will do my best to uphold the law of the land, even if there is a ghastly repeat of that business with the Ecquadorean activists, the nine fire extinguishers and the Wilkes-Barre Christmas Pageant.   *June, 1985*

BULLISH ON AMERICA

About a week before my well-earned vacation, I wrote a somewhat controversial column about the Reagan administration and South Africa, and the policies of the former concerning the latter. I alleged that Mr. Reagan was a mental midget and his policies were an ethical toxic waste site.

"The morals of a bat in heat" is the phrase I used to describe Mr. Reagan in this regard.

The accuracy of these observations is not in question. Two weeks after it was written, the President said in an interview that segregation does not exist in South Africa. The next day, the official White House Explainers stated that, when Reagan said that segregation does not exist in South Africa, he actually meant that segregation does exist in South Africa.

A problem of semantics.

Despite my rigorous adherence to the truth, I was inundated with letters accusing me of despicable and unpatriotic behavior. "How dare you?" asked more than one writer. "You're a disgrace to your profession and your newspaper," wrote prominent residents of our wealthier suburbs.

And yet (as more sensitive readers realized) I was performing nothing less than my sacred patriotic duty as a citizen. By making intemperate remarks about the President, I was merely upholding the Constitution.

Return with us now to those thrilling days of yesteryear, when the first 10 amendments to the Constitution were made part of the prime document of American democracy.

I refer specifically to that portion of the First Amendment that requires Congress to make no law abridging the freedom of the press.

Why is that in there? Is it to protect me when I write charming anecdotes about my rosebushes? It is not.

Is it to protect Peter Stack's witty interview with Lorna Stacey

Hoad, star of the new movie *St. Teresa's Stupid Younger Sister?* It is not.

Is it to protect editorial writers when, with elephantine delicacy, they opine that "the President may perhaps have acted overhastily when, through a regrettable error in communication, he decided blah blah genteel euphemism blah blah hedged opinion blah blah guarded dissent"?

Nope. These bits of prose do not need protection. They are trivial or reasoned or both; they can move in the best circles; they can agree to disagree.

It is the extreme attack, the ad hominem thrust, the rhetorical flourish, that require the stout wall of official tolerance. The antidote to bland official malfeasance is not bland cautious disagreement; it's the guy in the crowd jumping up and down and yelling "naked, the guy's starkers, a loathsome idiot worm pretending to be a statesman, impeach him right now."

A columnist can write about almost anything; the only time the Constitution cares is when he attacks the people in power in the strongest possible terms. "He can do that," says the Constitution. "He's supposed to do that," says the Constitution. "We want him to do that," says the Constitution.

So, as a strict constructionist, I felt that it was my Jeffersonian duty to remind my readers that Ronald Reagan is a thoroughgoing hypocrite seeking to promulgate a racist, pseudo-Christian philosophy.

Any other viewpoint is, I feel, unpatriotic.   *September, 1985*

WHAT MY COUNTRY MEANS TO ME

That was the old grammar school essay topic, was it not? Some gang of local patriots would give a $50 savings bond to the child who could string together the most impressive list of conventional sentiments about the Gem of the Ocean. Usually the essay contest was held in conjunction with the Fourth of July, a national holiday.

So it's the Fourth of July, and what does my country mean to me? More precisely, does my country mean anything to me? Does my nationality symbolize anything at all?

It certainly defines me, makes me eligible for certain benefits. It gives me an accent and a street address and a Social Security number.

And a mere glance around the globe indicates that, whatever my concerns and criticisms are, I am floating in the 99th percentile on the quality of life index, and that even the most wretched residents of the Bay Area are substantially better cared for than almost all of the residents of Somalia or Mongolia.

Here or Peru? Here or Romania? Here or Egypt? Here or Laos? No contest. We got it good, and that ain't bad.

In my heart, however, I believe that much of our current situation is the product of luck rather than virtue. Our land is large and fertile; we have space and topsoil. We're rapidly depleting both, but we're not really feeling it yet. And we have no ancient enmities, like those that cripple so many nations, no tribal hatreds running thousands of years deep.

So is that what America means to me? Just another hunk of real estate with a run of good luck heading for the big fall; a beautiful time frame; another lovely empire in a prerubble condition. Nope. All true, but not all there is.

America is not its politicians; that's good to remember. We did produce Thomas Jefferson and James Madison and Harry Truman; we also produced Millard Fillmore and Gerald Ford. Our leaders do seem to be getting worse, although I am aware that most people in most eras think their politicians are the utter dregs.

But who was surprised when George Bush reversed himself on taxes? Who is surprised when any politician lies? The problem is not the spirit of compromise; the problem is the initial promises. They lie to get elected, Democrats and Republicans alike. I assume if Libertarians got power they'd become liars and panderers too; it seems to be built into the system.

But built in by us. There's the rub. It's still a functioning democracy; the votes are honestly counted. It turns out (Jefferson and Madison would not be happy to hear this) that there are all kinds of tyranny, and the urge to manipulate power will adapt to changing circumstances.

But it's our buttons that are getting pushed; ain't nobody here but us dupes. The only reason that I continue to vote is that I don't want the system to wither away. The people I vote for (I use the Least Loathsome System) are, at best, a form of human riprap, protecting me from even viler manifestations of ambition and avarice.

These are the checks and balances we hear so much about: The fools protect us from the knaves, and knaves protect us from the fools.

And in the cracks, we get freedom. Freedom under siege, often freedom without justice, but nevertheless vast and lovely and constant.

It's hokey and oversimplified, but I believe it: As long as there is freedom, there is hope. New days dawn; things change. The reality is compromised, but the principle is still honored.

Mostly, the principle is still protected. Today, that's enough.

July, 1990

IN THE REIGN OF DOGS AND CATS

This is intelligent. This is truly smart and wonderful. Delta District Puppy Lovers, upset because living doggies and kitties are used in medical experiments, think it's a good idea to burn down a UC Davis veterinary laboratory.

This laboratory (should it ever be finished; there's a $2.5 million shortfall very likely because of puppy passion) would have been used to diagnose animal diseases. Bunnies and gerbils would have been returned to health because of the services offered in this building.

Ah, but returned to health in a corrupt society where living kitties are used in medical research. The line must be drawn somewhere, in this case in the dirt in front of the new veterinary science building.

Makes you proud to be a leftist, doesn't it?

Of course, the Puppy Lovers could have chosen to burn down another building. They could say it would be nice to burn down the local SPCA, where kitties are put to death every day of the year, just killed dead without any useful information being derived.

The kitties have to die because there is no one to feed them. They have to die because the people who claim to really care about kitties are too busy burning down science buildings to educate the populace at large about the necessity of sterilization for household pets.

Or they could opt for burning down the local fast-food outlet, where dead cows are grilled and eaten 18 hours a day. Presumably, those cows would rather have remained uneaten; that would have been an extremely liberating experience, in the terms that a cow can understand.

But probably such a cleansing fire would not gather public support. Hamburger joints and the SPCA are part of the sympathetic continuum. The University of California, sadly, is not.

Let me arrange my biases on the kitchen table. I am opposed to the torture of doggies and kitties, but I am far more opposed to the torture of human beings, whether by prison guards in South Africa or

143

interrogators in Moscow or landlords in Indonesia.

Animal liberation fans don't seem to have much time for their fellow humans. It's like an excuse for not having a social conscience. If we could halt the senseless slaughter of Iraqi teenagers and Salvadoran farmers and Chilean intellectuals, maybe I could worry a little bit harder about California pussycats.

If I could save either a human or a kitten from starvation, I would choose the human without hesitation.

I am species-centric. If it were my life against a human baby, I don't know what I'd do, but my life against a cat's life is easy. The cat feels the same way. It doesn't blame me; I don't blame it.

Now, suppose the only way a cure for AIDS could be found was by killing animals. I would support the killing of animals without hesitation. I know people who have died of AIDS; if 10,000 kitties had had to be sacrificed to prevent those deaths, I would be somewhat sad but mostly happy.

And that is the brutal necessity of medical research: It is necessary to use living tissue to study the progress of disease. It is necessary to examine the living tissue, which means killing the owner of same.

Just one planet here; we feed on each other; it's a circle of fixed dimensions. Certainly those who use animals for research should be monitored to make sure they do not make the animals suffer unnecessarily; beyond that . . . let 100 humans bloom.   *April, 1987*

WITH A GUN IN MY HAND

I've never met Jack Spiegelman, but I feel as though I know him. He is the father of a daughter; I am also a father of daughters. His daughter was close to the center of his life; I feel the same way about mine.

The difference is: His daughter was murdered in cold blood; mine, thank God, are still alive and prospering and lovely. I don't know what it would be like for me if that were not true, but I can imagine.

I did imagine.

I hope that I would have enough patience to wait until the murderer was tried in a court of law. But if (as happened to Jack Spiegelman) it took three years for Daniel David Morgan to come to trial, 36 months and still a large question about whether he would even be convicted, I can see myself buying a gun.

I don't know much about guns, but I can envision myself learning. I can imagine that I might try to sneak this pistol through the lax security at the San Francisco Hall of Justice. I can believe—I can believe with no effort at all—that I would fire this gun at the head of the man who murdered my daughter, entirely cognizant of the consequences and entirely indifferent to them.

If you rip the center out of my life, you pay. If you destroy innocence and hope, you pay. It's built into the genes; it flows in the blood.

Fall to the floor, writhe on the ground, scream and bellow, vomit blood, die. I'm serious.

And society must be protected from people like me.

That's the truth of it. My individual desire for revenge, no matter how justified, no matter how deeply felt, works against the continuity of civilization.

Dispassionate justice is better than vigilante justice. Not always more fair, certainly never as swift, but it protects us from ourselves; it allows us to live in dense communities without 50 percent of the population dying of homicide every year.

It ain't perfect, but it's better than the alternative: every man his own judge and jury; every man (including all the psychopaths and grief-struck relatives and nasty drunks and Stallone clones) his own executioner.

Rationality is not satisfying; it makes bad theater. But it's all we've got.

On the very day that Jack Spiegelman was pumping bullets into Daniel David Morgan, the House passed a bill (already, in essence, approved by the Senate) substantially weakening the 1968 Gun Control Act.

It did so against the strenuous objection of all law enforcement authorities. Some people tend to think of the cops as some domestic extension of the Defense Department, but this vote should bury that notion. Our elected representatives will earmark billions for some missile designed to kill foreigners, but not one cent for a bill designed to save the lives of American policemen.

Naked and nasty politics, in its purest and most distasteful form. Our elected representatives chose lust for votes over social responsibility. Restricting guns does not stop the rage to murder; it just makes the act more difficult. With a total ban on handguns, Daniel David Morgan might not be on trial; and Jack Spiegelman might be watching the culmination of another spring with his beloved daughter.

April, 1986

ORDINARY MIRACLES HAPPENING DAILY

The trouble is, there is too much kindness in the world; too much generosity of spirit; too much idealism. Find a church basement or a community center—there it is. So ordinary it's hardly a story.

Does seem a shame to disqualify all this strength and energy from media attention on the basis of "same old heartbreaking altruism—get me a new angle." So pick one. Pick the Family School, on Fillmore between Fell and Oak. You pass within 100 yards of it every time you roar up Fell on your way west. The Sacred Heart block. Sure.

Family School provides education for women on welfare. It also provides child care for women on welfare. Women from the projects; women with chemical dependency histories (although they have to be clean and stay clean to remain at Family School); women with family violence lurking in their pasts and futures.

The women study for a General Equivalency Diploma upstairs; the preschool kids are taken care of downstairs. This is not warehousing; the spaces for the children are all lovingly decorated, friendly and cluttered and optimistic.

An Equivalency Diploma is not a charitable credential given for trying hard and not talking in class. "I would maintain that our women have a better education than many of the high school graduates out there," said Rosemary Kelley, one of the ordinary idealists at Family School.

The Rev. Calvin Jones Jr., Baptist minister, director of the school, a graduate of the University of Washington with a master's from Harvard Divinity School, took the trigonometry part of the GED. He gave up after the fourth question. "Are you kidding?" he is reported to have said.

No one thinks that trigonometry is an essential life skill, but the knowledge that you can learn trigonometry is very useful indeed. The GED is definitely doing it the hard way; some employers give brownie points for that.

Loretta Payne has only math to go on the GED. Meanwhile, she's starting City College in the fall, trying to begin a career as an occupational therapist. She has been at Family School three years; her 2-year-old child has been enrolled downstairs for six months.

Payne is 28, African-American, lives in the neighborhood. She has two daughters; the older one is 10. She lives on $630 a month plus food stamps. And she's willing to do sines and cosines if that's what it takes.

Isn't this the hot methodology now, getting people off the welfare rolls and onto the payrolls? Aren't we as a society investing our plentiful resources in these kinds of worthy programs?

Not so's you'd notice. Says Jones: "$3,400 keeps a woman enrolled here for a year. Costs $30,000 to take that same woman and lock her up for using crack. One guess where the money's going."

Downstairs is one of the preschool teachers, Sharon Bryar. BA in philosophy from Boston College, advanced degree in early childhood education. Been with Family School since its inception five years ago.

Works 8- to 10-hour days, much time after school spent on the computer twisting her way through the maze of ever-changing funding regulations.

Salary: $24,000, up from $22,000. What she's really making, of course, is a difference.

The Family School needs money. Did that point come across? About $450 a month would sponsor a child in the nursery; $550 in the preschool program. Write them a letter (548 Fillmore, San Francisco 94117).* Some miracles still available.   *July, 1990*

*This address is still accurate. I know you didn't expect to be hit up for money in the middle of a book, but you were anyway.

SOMETIMES I FEEL LIKE
A CHILDLESS MOTHER

Today's heroines are Sue Pavlik and Millie Jessen, the women who recently won their fight to adopt Eric, a two-year-old child with AIDS.

Well, right. In a society somewhat better designed than this one, the idea of having to fight to win the right to care for a sick, unwanted child would be foolish, even cruel. Children require love: This is a widely acknowledged fact.

But Sue Pavlik and Millie Jessen are lesbians. They practice the Love That Dare Not Speak Its Name, Not That Name, The Other One. So the sick, unwanted child has to be warehoused somewhere while the state goes through a massive, convulsive hoo-hah about whether or not lesbians should be allowed to care for children.

Here's the dilemma once again: Should a sick child get care of erratic quality in a series of short-term foster homes, or should a sick child get loving, reliable care in a permanent home? That's a tough one, isn't it?

Does the child get a vote?

But Sue Pavlik and Millie Jessen persevered, and that's why they're heroines.

Think of what they went through: They decided to take on an AIDS baby in the first place. There's not exactly a boom market in the little rascals. Then they had to decide to go public with their sexual orientation, an exquisitely private matter.

(Remember, a significant number of people in this country think that being a lesbian is so awful that it disqualifies you from caring for a needy child. Going public is big juju; the labels stick, the ghosts rise.)

And then they had the legal battle.

Here's what they were up against: Jim Brown is the chief of adoptions for the California Department of Social Services, which has a rule against adoptions by gay and lesbian couples. (It was judicial, not administrative, action that allowed the adoption.) Brown supports that rule:

"We can get into these really crazy situations. It's possible to have a large number of parents created in this process. I do know of at least some children who have at least three mothers."

Uh-oh. Three mothers. So messy around holiday time, and all those nagging phone calls. . . .

The point is that there are thousands and thousands of babies—particularly black or mixed-race babies, particularly disabled babies, particularly sick babies—who don't have any mothers at all. Nice healthy white babies get to live with Glenn Close and James Woods and see the tree with the white flowers every spring (*Immediate Family*—a movie), but other baby flavors are not popular.

And then you get a couple who says, "We'd like one of those babies," and the California Department of Social Services says, "Wait a minute! What have you been doing in the bedroom?" So useful, don't you think?

One further thing: It seems a spiritual exercise of considerable dimensions to take on a baby with AIDS, that is, to take on a baby with a fatal disease.

All parents know that their children are going to die; it is one of the great blessings of parenthood that usually we get to die before our kids do. We take that as the final solace, the tragedy that will happen without us.

It seems probable that this will not be true for Sue Pavlik and Millie Jessen. It seems probable that they have accepted that as unselfishly and courageously as they have accepted Eric himself. It seems probable that their decision enriches us all.

November, 1989

PREDATORY LESBIANS BEHIND THE BULKHEADS

Thanks to the good reporting of Jane Gross of the *New York Times*, we know now that the U.S. Navy officially believes that the lesbians in its command tend to be "hard-working, career-oriented sailors" who should be identified and fired as rapidly as possible.

The all-heterosexual Navy. I feel safer already.

Why should lesbians be separated from service regardless of their competence? Because, according to a memorandum written by Vice Admiral Joseph S. Donnell, "the presence of such members adversely affects the ability of the armed forces to maintain discipline, good order and morale."

Lesbians, it seems, have an "adverse impact" on those "who must live and work in close proximity" to them. They create a "predator-type environment" in which "more senior and aggressive female sailors" exert "subtle coercion" and make "outright sexual advances" on their "young, often vulnerable" female colleagues.

No evidence is produced to back up this claim; this is not social science, this is fear-driven chunky drivel. Last year, the Pentagon prepared two studies that showed that homosexuals do not disrupt the armed forces; these studies were suppressed. But let's look at it anyway; there's some interesting stuff going on.

Now these predatory lesbians. Let us assume with Vice Admiral Donnell (which vice is he admiral of?—that's a joke you won't find in this column) that the voting-age women who choose a career in the armed forces are indeed shrinking flowers of Victorian womanhood ripe for gin-swilling below-decks diesel dykes.

So "outright sexual advances" are made. Perhaps there is a moment of maidenly refusal; nevertheless, the innocent young sailor is overpowered. It is not my belief that lesbian rape is a growing social problem, but let's say that it is. What then? Well, it's assault. It's a crime. I have every confidence that the Navy would vigorously prosecute such a crime.

I suspect that Donnell is not worried about assault; I suspect he's worried about consensual behavior. It sounds as if he believes that sexual orientation is something you vote on, like what movie to show in the mess hall.

Get one silver-tongued talker holding little educational seminars, and pretty soon all the gals will be dating other gals. What of the gene pool?

Nevertheless, there's a real concern at the heart of all this homophobia. When sex and romance get tangled up in the workplace, there's likely to be various kinds of trouble: preferential treatment, jealousy, long sulks and long sighs, manipulation of assignments, you name it.

Certainly happens in the heterosexual corporate world; no reason why it wouldn't happen in a lesbian environment just as much. But here's the thing: In the military, just as in any huge organization, there are dozens of power games and alliances outside the organizational chart: trading on friendships or old school ties or family connections, technical blackmail and moral extortion, protection rackets of all kinds, pandering, flattery, bonding.

Things would certainly be more efficient without it, but there it is. I assume that Sappho-Americans are not immune from these pressures. Sex makes it more complicated; no question. But as long as male heterosexual sailors visit whorehouses together—and are issued condoms by the Navy before they leave ship—it seems to me lesbians should be allowed to serve without fear of official harassment.

September, 1990

WITHIN THE CONTEXT OF BAD CONTEXT

It was a telephone conversation with a colleague, a friend of a friend, a man I had almost met half a dozen times. We were having a tentative professional conversation about matters of, as they say, mutual interest.

There was a lot of banter; there usually is between us colorful, wise-cracking media types. At one point we were talking about Frank Capra movies.

"That would be fine with me," I said. "I'd love to be in a movie where I overcome great obstacles through my basic human decency and receive the plaudits of a grateful community. A grateful community of beautiful women would be even better."

There was the slightest of pauses, and then the conversation moved on. Ten minutes later, off on another tangent, he said, "My lover and I both would be interested. He really likes things like that."

So began the internal dialogue, wondering whether I had said anything wrong, whether he had heard me say anything wrong even if I hadn't, wondering whether this agonizing was not a form of pathology . . . a straight guy makes a joke about having a fantasy about beautiful women to a gay guy. So?

Without an answer, I called him back. "Mumble sputter you know ha ha," I remarked. "I didn't mean to be exclusionary mumble sputter."

"I thought about it," he said evenly, "and I figured it was your fantasy. If I'd thought you needed your consciousness raised, I would have said something." Round of good-byes repeated; phone call ended.

So what? So give me a gold star I'm sensitive? So give me a black star I'm too damn delicate for words? Worth thinking about, anyway.

Here's what I thought: I am as annoyed as anyone by this whole tidal wave of political correctness, this avalanche of tortured bureaucratic phrases ("genetically challenged"; "chronologically gifted") to describe subsets of humans, this growing list of outlawed thoughts and words and speculations.

I do believe that there are professional whiners, tiny tyrants of disability and disadvantage, who persist in turning every issue into the same issue, in narrowing all human experience into a single dynamic, which is how the system is designed to make them feel bad.

And I do believe that there is an entire generation of academics who have turned their traditional fear and hatred of the gritty, vivid world outside the academy into a gigantic hierarchy of oppression with which they belabor their students and harass their colleagues.

But what I had not realized until just now is that the real problem with all this wailing about political correctness is that it is profoundly desensitizing. We learn the words and forget the reason; our smugness goes through the roof as our understanding plummets.

People are still being denied the comforts of religion, of legal marriage, of ordinary acceptance, because of their sexual orientation.

Hell, there are still people being beaten bloody.

And there is still the easy assumption by the majority that everyone is like them, is heterosexual. I know because there is that easy assumption within me, and I am as sensitive as all get-out. What a drag it must be to be gay and have to process all remarks through a goodwill filter. "He probably didn't realize" or "I'm sure that was unintentional" or whatever. No wonder there's a temptation to just start stepping on toes, if only to give your own feet a rest for a while.

Screw political correctness; think common courtesy. It's on the human scale that the real work of tolerance gets done.

November, 1990

LEARNING TO THINK RAMBUNCTIOUSLY

Somewhat in spite of myself, my cultural heroine of the moment is Camille Paglia, author of *Sexual Personae: Art and Decadence from Nefertiti to Emily Dickinson* and dispenser of good-humored outrage in better media outlets everywhere.

Our text for this morning is a remark by her during an interview published in Harper's magazine. "Some people are inclined to the sedentary life that reading requires," she said, "but others are not. That is why the entire discourse on sex and gender in academe and in the media is so off, because teachers and writers are not nearly as athletic or rambunctious as others."

Deliciously wicked, yes? It is not something, in my experience, that media workers stand around the coffee machine talking about— "you know, I'm not so hot in the sack; how about you?"—and it may not even be true. The evidence is mixed.

But it is certainly true that since sex became a fit topic for public discourse, it has been hijacked by the people in charge of discourse. It has generated experts and polemicists; it has become a social issue, a political issue, a medical issue, a moral issue.

Meanwhile, at the level of life outside discourse, sex has gone on being irreducible and confusing and wonderful and nonverbal. The actual experts are still dancers and bankers and nurses and unemployed sheetrockers; anyone who has not let theory get in the way of practice.

Sex still belongs to the rambunctious. Hooray for the good guys.

Image magazine last Sunday ran a long piece on lesbian power in San Francisco that included an interview with the wonderful Susie Bright, the editor of *On Our Backs* ("Entertainment for the Adventurous Lesbian").

Bright was quoted describing a stereotype of lesbian behavior: "On the one hand, there was oral sex in an egalitarian manner. You know, I'll lick you for 10 minutes and you lick me for 10 minutes, and there won't be any penetration because that's male oriented, and I won't look at your breasts more than just in passing because that would be objectifying, and we won't talk dirty to each other and we won't sweat."

What is remarkable about the quote is not that it's graphic (in this age of AIDS, there have been far franker discussions in the popular media) but that it is worldly.

Worldly is not an attribute of most of the discussions of sex and gender in the media, or in academic papers. These discussions seem to come from and describe a hermetic universe fundamentally unrelated to the world of experience.

It sometimes makes for a parlor game of a rather high order—Find the Patriarchy, for instance, or Cleanse Your Sexual Preferences—but it doesn't have much to do with what happens at the level of neurons and blood flow. But the young, you know—the young are impressionable. The young may somehow think that they are required to trivialize their erotic impulses by straining them through the unforgiving sieve of politics. That would be too bad—no one should be having a crabbed, hesitant time in the sack in the service of a faddish set of half-baked ideas.

But not to worry: The life-affirming revisionists are everywhere among us, refusing to declare the end of civilization, refusing to confuse politics with life.

Being worldly; loving the world; loving the impulse and the moment. There's room for that still.

March, 1991

THEY'RE NOT ANGELS; THESE AREN'T PINS

I love a good medieval dispute as much as the next sentient being, but I am nevertheless a bit sad to see the letters column of this newspaper fill up once again with a dispute between prolife and prochoice advocates over When Life Begins.

It's a theological argument. There is no final evidence, no "proof." The virgin birth; 431 angels on the head of a pin; that moment at which the spark of existence is struck—all matters of faith. You may believe whatever feels comfortable.

But whatever you believe, it's unwise to make public policy based on it. Church goes in this box; state goes in that box. It's not just a good idea; it's the law.

So let us for the moment clear away the underbrush. Let us stipulate that life begins the moment the little eyeless polliwog enters the Magic Circle. Let's say that this little featureless cell, unnoticed by its host, is in fact a living being. Let's get off the Trimester Treadmill.

And let's talk about AK-47s.

An AK-47 is for shooting people. Brave young men do not go into the rolling woodlands of America searching for tasty venison with AK-47s strapped to their backs. If the medium is the message, the message of the AK-47 is: Bang bang, you're dead.

So it would seem to me that, if one were "prolife," one would also be anti-AK-47. In fact, a really comprehensive "prolife" movement would probably include literature concerning the topic.

But somehow, you know, it doesn't. Somehow, certain sentimental, philosophically indefensible notions about "innocence" seem to hang over the prolife crowd like a damp mist. The unspoken assumption seems to be: As soon as a being hits the air and begins sinning in one way or another, it loses its claim on our concern.

By the time it's old enough to go to grade school, it's lost its charm. By the time it's old enough to bear children, we are able to ignore it entirely. A hierarchy is established, a hierarchy with the unborn at the top of the pyramid.

Tyrant babies.

Same deal with nuclear weapons.* Nuclear weapons are designed to kill people; kill a bunch of them immediately and then a lot more later. You'd think that a "prolife" movement might be in favor of banning nuclear weapons.

But somehow, you know, it isn't.

That's because nuclear weapons are designed to kill our enemies. But if we've learned one thing in the last 20 years, it's that the "enemies" nuclear weapons are designed to kill are more or less people like us, merchants and mothers and poets and grandfathers and vegetarians and bums, and that they are our enemies only because their government is mad at our government.

In fact, it is possible to argue that those little innocent unwanted babies growing inside the bellies of unknowing mothers represent far more of a danger to our society than some corporal from Minsk.

An unwanted child harms both itself and its mother. Sometimes love can conquer this handicap, but often it can't, and then there is anguish, violence, crime, the whole urban cycle of despair that begins with too many hungry babies. But "prolife" folks seem indifferent to this difficulty; they're having too much fun hassling pregnant women at Planned Parenthood centers.

You'd think that a "prolife" movement might be opposed to terrorizing women who are exploring every option while attempting to make a private and difficult choice. But somehow, you know, it isn't.

February, 1989

Many readers will remember the Cold War.

SETTING UP A STRAW PERSON

Why does anyone want to be a political candidate? Worst job in the world, exceeded only by the job the political candidate is so desperately seeking to achieve. Terrible hours, constant abuse, round-the-clock hypocrisy, pitfalls lurking at every turn.

That's what happened to our Ms. Feinstein, I believe. She had just answered 5,735 questions correctly and was all set to handle the 5,736th when she made a fatal error: She stopped to think. Campaigning has nothing to do with thinking; campaigning has to do with repeating bland slogans.

If you don't repeat bland slogans, tempests in teapots ensue. DiFi was asked what she thought about abortion based solely on the sex of the child, and she considered the question. That fatal spark of intelligence betrayed her. Gee, she thought, as most of us would, that sounds pretty creepy. I'd hate to think that was going on. So she said she'd consider a law banning it. Then a day later, she said she wouldn't. Not exactly her finest hour. She will be asked about it every day between now and June 5. This is known as the Quemoy-Matsu Effect. It's one of the 32 major reasons voter apathy is so rampant.

Quemoy and Matsu, readers will recall, are two tiny islands between Taiwan and the Chinese mainland. Nobody gave a rat's rump about them until the Kennedy-Nixon debates of 1960, at which time they became a symbol of appeasement. Was Kennedy, Nixon wanted to know, prepared to lose Quemoy and Matsu to the Godless Communists?

Once the election was over, Quemoy and Matsu dropped from public debate. They may have actually sunk into the ocean. In terms other than the context of a political campaign, they were insignificant to American policy.

And so we have abortions on the basis of sex. Oh, darn, it's a girl; better abort it. The point is: There is no evidence that this is happening in the United States. China, yes; India, yes; here, no.

Americans don't think like that.

(This is not to say that an American woman has never decided to have an abortion on the basis of the sex of the child she was carrying. Indeed, it is certain that, somewhere, sometime, an American mother has decided to abort a child because it interfered with her prepaid trip to Hawaii. Freedom of choice is like freedom of speech; not all the consequences are benign.)

It's as though DiFi had been asked: What are you going to do about widows hurling themselves on their husbands' funeral pyres? Shouldn't that be outlawed? It's a nonissue in the Western Hemisphere.

So why was it brought up at all? Because it is part of the national right-to-life strategy. In states like California, where tough Idaho-style antiabortion legislation doesn't have a chance of passing, the right-to-lifers have decided to push for milder forms of legislation.

Many of these involve consent issues: a law mandating that a woman must get parental or spousal consent before getting an abortion. The point is to establish the precedent that the state has the right to decide under what circumstances a woman may have an abortion.

Sex selection is another one of those. Never mind that it's unenforceable; never mind that it fixes something that ain't broke. Get it on the books and build a mighty edifice on the principle it embodies.

I have no opinion on the candidates—the debate made me dislike both of them about equally—but I do feel sorry for DiFi. She'd better learn to mouth clichés every waking moment, or it'll be the Doughboy versus the Invisible Man come November.* *July 1990*

Editor's note: The Invisible Man won. We call him Governor Wilson now.

SPIN CONTROL: STILL A GROWTH INDUSTRY

Just this week in San Francisco there occurred a large, private meeting of various bigwigs in the Bishops' Committee for Pro-Life Activities, which is the antiabortion activist arm of the Roman Catholic Church.

The members of the committee were here to plot details of a $5 million media campaign. Curiously, the members of the committee were surprised that their little meeting drew media attention. Had they realized they were going to get media attention, they could have delivered eloquent prepared statements instead of looking like startled raccoons in the glare of television lights.

Still, off-the-cuff statements can be revealing. Suzanne Harvath, a psychologist and Catholic antiabortion official with the Archdiocese of St. Louis, was asked about the purpose of the meeting. "Our message is not getting the right spin," she said.

Somehow, I don't think that's the problem. Saddam Hussein, now—Saddam Hussein has a spin problem, at least in this country. Most Americans have little interest in or knowledge of Iraq, Kuwait or the historical flux of power in the Muslim world.

Therefore, in forming their judgments, most Americans must pick between competing images rather than competing realities.

Is Hussein a mad butcher? Many would now say yes. Was he a mad butcher in 1985, when we were supporting him against Iran? Maybe so, but he had better spin doctors. It is useful to remember that whatever our opinions on the Iraq situation, they are really just decisions about the trustworthiness of various sources of information.

We do not know what is going on. If previous dynamics hold, we will find out much later what was actually going on, and we will be surprised.

But abortion is different. Almost everyone has been touched directly by the issue at some level. Most people have been involved in a decision to have (or to refrain from having) an abortion. Perhaps there was quarreling; perhaps the outcome of that decision has strained or broken family ties.

And there are the movies of the fetuses, and the unwanted children on the street or in institutions, and the harangues from the pulpit or the political platform. There is no issue more visible; there is no issue taken more seriously; there is no issue less in need of spin control.

Both sides are still trying, of course. "Prolife" and "prochoice"—is there anything more irritating than those terms? Image mongering with human life. Say the word: Abortion. Proabortion, antiabortion. That's the issue; the rest is just self-serving rhetoric.

And this week the antiabortionists sat around the Cathedral Hill hotel listening to the international public relations firm of Hill & Knowlton make a pitch for the biz. I see something tasteful, Your Eminence. Remember the early ads for Infiniti?

You know what would make me happy? Might make a few million other people happy, too. If all these bishops and feminists and consultants and legislators could start a dialogue based on mutual accommodation and mutual respect, then maybe we could stop yelling at each other.

No one wants unwanted pregnancies—that's the common ground; maybe we could start there. Solve the problem before it becomes a problem. Maybe we could control the spin in that neighborhood for a while.

I don't know the answer. I do know that as long as the Bishops' Committee insists on selling religious philosophy like a personal grooming aid, we're moving further away from rationality and reconciliation.

August, 1990

THE AFTERMATH OF AFTERMATH

Lately, I have been playing a nasty little game with myself: How many disasters am I away from homelessness? Between two or three is the answer I usually come up with, although that answer is based partly on my utterly inadequate understanding of the provisions of my various insurance policies.

That is not comforting. I used not to think about disaster at all, except as an occasional entree on the news menu. It was a thing, it happened, it had metaphorical weight and great visual appeal.

Not this year.

In the last couple of days, the news has been dull; my tastes have become jaded. Yes, the economy's getting worse and Yugoslavia seems to be eating its own entrails and nearly half the high school students in Oakland have a D or F average, but where's the hot stuff? Did any international celebrity announce that he has HIV? Was there a billion-dollar fire in my neighborhood? Are any Supreme Court nominees lying on television today? Are we at war again? How about an earthquake?

No? Then I'll sit today out. I know there'll be another crisis along any minute now. Programming will be preempted, traffic will be rerouted, troops will be deployed, all citizens will be asked to read the following announcement.

The Gulf War was in this calendar year, friends. Remember the Gulf War? Sort of like Vietnam only more recent. The details may have slipped your mind.

And the Soviet Union collapsed. Please make a note of it for your files.

I'd heard about future shock, but I never thought it would happen to me. Are we to expect this pace of crisis mongering for the rest of the century?

I keep thinking that, in 50 years, popular historians will be writing books called *1991: Crucible of Change* or *The Year of Living Nuttily.*

Assuming there are popular historians; assuming there are books.

It's the year of the Big Empty. There's a hole in the center of everything; there are no safe places. Maybe this is reality, but it feels like Mars.

Do people believe in things any more? I'm not talking about the things so much as I am about the belief itself. I understand that people have attached themselves to causes, but do these attachments spring from principles? Largely, it seems not; largely, it seems like dogma.

I am not confident that the distinction between "dogma" and "principles" is a real one anymore.

I understand that every age thinks of itself as the apocalyptic fulcrum of the future; I understand that nostalgia for the good old days is always with us and always inaccurate.

I also understand that this is conventional wisdom, and that conventional wisdom is also wrong. I can picture a liberal philosopher in Cambodia as the Khmer Rouge began its appalling slaughter—"Sure, but you know, these things blow over." The Khmer Rouge is still part of the Cambodian government. Used to be, you killed one million people, you didn't get to hold office for a while.

It is a given that people get more quarrelsome and cranky as they get older; I feel about 112 right now. But I don't notice any optimistic young people saying, "Buck up, gramps, the future is in safe hands."

Instead, I notice cross-generational despair. I notice people wincing before the next blow is struck; I notice people checking their canned goods. We are not renters or owners anymore; we are merely the temporarily housed.   *November, 1991*

IT'S TIME AGAIN FOR THE UNTIED WAY

The Untied Way is not the perfect charity. For one thing, it is not, strictly speaking, a charity at all. It has neither a street address nor a fax number; it has no long-range strategy or targeted marketing plan. It does not have a prestigious advisory board nor fund-raising galas for that board to attend. It does not even have a large plywood thermometer indicating the pace of contributions.

It cannot provide long-term counseling services or purchase expensive medical equipment. It cannot do follow-up studies or create pie charts. Nevertheless, it has a place in the patchwork of the wealth-distribution network.

The Untied Way has no overhead; 100 percent of the money reaches the people who need it. The Untied Way has no criteria for need; it assumes that the people who are wandering the streets asking for money are doing so because they actually need money.

There may be millionaires using this method to increase their liquid assets, but the Untied Way does not believe so. People who stand on cold street corners wearing signs saying "Homeless — Please Help" are almost certainly homeless and in need of help.

It is very possible that the people who are funded by the Untied Way will spend their money in unwise ways. Perhaps they will buy cheap booze or illegal drugs; perhaps they will gamble it away. The Untied Way regrets that this is so, but believes that charity, like justice, is blind.

Besides, Untied Way volunteers have been known to spend money unwisely themselves; not to allow others the same freedom would seem hypocritical. More empathy and fewer opinions; the Untied Way urges that point of view.

Put it like this: The Untied Way allows its clients to apply their cash grants to self-identified need areas.

How does it work? An Untied Way volunteer (and you, reading this very fine collection of columns right now, are a potential Untied

Way volunteer) goes to his or her ATM and withdraws a sum of money.

We suggest $100 or 1/500th of your annual income, whichever is greater. Nice crisp $20 bills add to the holiday cheer, but limp sodden $20 bills are also OK.

Having withdrawn the money, the Untied Way volunteer (very possibly yourself) proceeds to an area of town populated by the seriously underfunded. The Untied Way volunteer walks down the street. With luck, people will ask the volunteer for money. The volunteer hands each person who asks a $20 bill. The volunteer continues in this mode until all the money is gone.

That is the Untied Way.

Should you choose to become a volunteer, you may be thanked for your efforts. On the other hand, you may not. Some Untied Way clients are extremely ungrateful. They may even wonder where you were when the box factory went out of business.

The box factory going out of business is not your fault, but you may be unable to make an effective case for that view. Remember the Founding Principle of the Untied Way: Gratitude is not the point.

Charity is the point. The Untied Way is a fine liberal organization; it believes that if you throw money at a problem, it will get better, at least for a little bit.

So put a smile on your face and an ATM card in your hand and go out there and start giving heedlessly. A little bit is never enough, but it is always more than nothing: That is the guiding philosophy of the Untied Way.*

A variant of this column has run every December since 1985; anecdotal reports (the Untied Way has no other kind) indicate that the number of volunteers grows yearly.

SECTION SIX

My Travels and Preoccupations

MY EVENING WITH GORDON AND ANN

When my trashy, low-life friends (perhaps I should say "former friends") discovered that I was dropping by Gordon and Ann Getty's place last week, their reactions could not have been more inappropriate.

"Count the servants," said one. "Be sure to go to the bathroom," said another. "Ask to see the egg," said a third.

"What egg?" I asked.

"They have a Faberge egg," said my friend.

Maybe they do and maybe they don't—I wouldn't know. The thing about me and the Gettys is, I don't really care about the money side of it at all. I don't even know what number richest man Gordon is. Maybe he's the world's 5th richest man, maybe the world's 22nd richest man—heck, he could be the world's 63rd richest man and it wouldn't make any difference to me.

So it was not vulgar curiosity that led me to the gracious Getty home that evening. No indeed, it was my deep commitment to physical anthropology, a commitment that began at an intense level a week ago Monday and continues unabated.

There is the Institute of Human Origins, a very well known and

167

worthy institute of which the Gettys are particularly fond. It's the somethingth anniversary of this very fine institute, and a few of the more decorative members of the press were invited to a tiny celebration to kick off a weekend of parties and banquets and requests for contributions. Also, they invited me. No doubt word had reached them of my almost total immersion in the study of the origins of human life. We are, in a very real sense, where we came from. The Gettys certainly believe that.

I am unable to reveal the precise location of the Getty home. I am allowed to say that it is not in Oakland. We pulled up at the large home in not-Oakland at precisely 6:50. The party was 6 to 8; we wanted to be neither early nor late.

A man in a white coat opened the car door. "Good evening, sir," he said, and handed me a ticket. My wife and I stood in the street gazing at the very wide facade of the home in front of us.

"Which door is it?" I asked casually. The man in the white coat pointed. We shared a merry laugh.

A large door; one would expect a large door. A prompt answer; one would expect a prompt answer. We stood in the foyer. There were two knots of people; both knots ignored us. We stood in the foyer some more. "Nice walls," I said to my wife.

Later, I would deny that I said "Nice walls."

Finally, a woman came up to us. "I'm Something, with the Gettys," she said. She actually said her name, but I was far too cool and relaxed to take notes. "They're all down there." She pointed down a marble hall that started at our toes and ended in Klamath Falls, Oregon.

We walked down the cold hall. To our left, an enclosed courtyard, vaguely Italian. We heard voices. At the end of the hall, we turned toward the voices. We entered the room.

A man with his back to us was speaking. He was thanking his good friend Gordon. His good friend Gordon was standing next to him.

Everyone was looking at us, because we were just behind the speaker. We had blundered into the spotlight like confused rabbits on a country lane unexpectedly frozen in the glare of headlights.

We smiled weakly and started sidling. We sidled next to Jerry Brown, known Democrat. "Mursh fooble," whispered Jerry Brown. "Leez," I replied. Houston, we have contact.

There was a lot of furniture. It was a very large room, but even for a large room it had a lot of furniture. Also, there was art. There was a Degas on one wall; opposite it was a Chinese screen perhaps 17 feet long and 8 feet tall. There was a lot of other art as well, art I myself could not identify, although I was sure it was art. The difference between the Getty home and a museum is that in the Getty home there are no helpful labels on the wall.

Some of the furniture was also art. All the furniture, crowded in with all the people who were sincerely dedicated to the Institute of Human Origins and were in no way merely there to check out the furniture, made for a somewhat congested conversation pit.

The speech was over soon enough. It was a very civilized speech and almost certainly very important. Then it was time to mingle. Mingling was difficult, due to the furniture glut.

Ann Getty had a secret path, a narrow opening between the gilded French mirror and the small French coffee table. She snaked through it covertly, avoiding a clotted mass of scientists. That's why when you're too rich, you can't be too thin—you have to be able to maneuver around the furniture.

We mingled in a stationary sort of way. We utilized our opposable thumbs to grasp drinks. We found ourselves in a conversation circle with Dianne Feinstein, her husband Dick Blum and the selfsame Jerry Brown.

The thing to know about these people is that they are large people. Dianne Feinstein is bigger than you think she is, broader and deeper and more solid. Dick Blum is huge, almost as huge as Gordon Getty himself, who is seriously huge. Jerry Brown is developing the shape of a plutocrat in a Thomas Nast cartoon.

As we were talking to these large people about small things, women with canapes circled the room. The canape trays had a separate silver bowl for the used toothpicks. For some reason, this fact powerfully excited me. You can take the boy out of the 'burbs, but you can't take the 'burbs out of the boy.

Men came by with trays, asking for drink orders. I selected Diet Coke; I wanted to get really wired without the annoying food value of sugar. Every time a man brought me a drink, he brought me a paper napkin. He made me take the napkin.

I have no idea what I'm supposed to do with a napkin when I'm standing up drinking a soda. Eventually, half-consciously, I wadded it up and put it in my pocket. Another drink, another napkin, another wad.

By the end of the party, I was noticeably listing to starboard, the victim of crumpled napkin overload.

Eventually, I had to go to the bathroom. It was out of genuine need and not vulgar curiosity. I asked someone where it was. "Go up the stairs," she said, "and take a left at the maid."

I went up the stairs. At the top of the stairs was a bulky man. His mouth was smiling, but his eyes were not. "Can I help you?" he asked softly.

"I am not a journalist and have no intention of writing about the Getty bathroom," I almost said. I would have meant every word. Wild horses could not drag from me so much as the design on the wallpaper.

OK: parrots.

SPACE ALIENS ARE MISUNDERSTOOD

I have a friend who has a friend who believes that she is a space alien. This is not the easiest burden in life to bear. Worrying about dental work is hard enough; being a space alien worrying about dental work can really get on a person's nerves.

Understand, this is a person who leads a full, active earthling life. She holds a job, buys groceries, has relationships, drives a car, has opinions on popular movies, plays tennis, travels to Seattle to visit her sister. She is not under the care of a physician other than her family doctor, who wants her to cut down on cholesterol.

But she believes that she is a space alien.

She doesn't tell many people that she is a space alien. Space aliens quickly learn that it is a bad idea to talk about it much. People don't understand. They try to talk you out of it. They advise you to seek professional help.

She doesn't want professional help. She is entirely aware that people who think they're space aliens are supposed to be crazy. It is not an honorable job classification, being a space alien.

So, as a thinking adult, she has been forced to ask herself: Am I crazy? She has considered the matter carefully; she has talked it over with a few trusted friends. And her conclusion: I am not crazy. I am only a space alien.

Right now, she just wants to know what being a space alien is supposed to entail. This differentiates her from many people who believe they are space aliens and are very busy following orders.

But she is not one of those people. She does not exhibit the classic clinical symptoms. She does not believe people are following her; she does not believe in the existence of a gigantic conspiracy designed to drive her crazy. She does not believe that Henry Kissinger is stealing her ideas.

If anything, she wishes the Mother Ship or whatever would be a little more forthcoming about its plans. She's tried listening for messages. She does believe that earthlings are slowly poisoning their planet, an idea shared by many people who do not believe that they are space aliens.

The alien chain of command is definitely nonfunctional from her point of view.

It's sort of like being given an office and a desk and being told that you're a corporate vice president, and then sitting there for years and years wondering what your job is and what the firm that employs you does.

Plus, you can't talk about it because people will think of you as some sort of *National Enquirer* fruitcake.

The more I heard about my friend's friend, the underemployed space alien, the more her plight sounded familiar. We were none of us in class the day they passed out the secret of life; we all of us wander around listening for messages that never seem to arrive. The only people who really screw up are the ones who think they've gotten the message. All those guys over the years who were convinced they had the exact date when the world would end—they're batting 0-for-eternity so far.

So here we are spinning through the unutterable void without a road map, bolstered only by the evidence of things not seen, bookended by the mysteries of birth and death, bewildered by our own emotions. . . . Talk about space aliens.

This is not your father's Oldsmobile. This might not even be a car.

AMAZING ADVANCES IN MODERN MEDICINE

According to a recent article submitted to the *New England Journal of Medicine,* researchers at several leading institutions have confirmed a "Yo-Yo Effect" in articles published in the *New England Journal of Medicine.*

Editors at the *New England Journal of Medicine* were all the way across the country and probably would not have responded to questions.

Dr. Hansel Glock of the National Institutes of Research told a packed press conference that the phenomenon "stands to reason. If we had been looking for it, we would have discovered it a long time ago. It's just one of those quirks of science, like the way people you knew in high school seem to develop puffy faces and really odd opinions."

Glock unveiled an elaborate analytical model called the What Kills You Matrix. The model was about four feet tall and made of a glossy blue plastic with highlights of amber and dusty rose. The veil itself was done in eggshell and beige with an intricately worked teal border.

"Suppose this is fats," said Glock, pointing to an area of the model. "Let's say that we have an article, perhaps even a *syndrome* or an *interdependent system* of articles, alleging that fats kill you very badly. Maybe half the magazine, something like that.

"So next month, the *New England Journal of Medicine* would definitely not publish another article saying that fats kill you. That would be foolish and repetitious. But it would publish an article saying that fats don't kill you. And then, a few months later, an article saying wait a minute, yes they do. And so forth.

"It's the Yo-Yo Effect."

But what, Glock was asked, is the effect of his revelations on the average citizen?

"I believe that my findings validate the Stopped Clock Lifestyle. This is the lifestyle I now recommend to all my patients."

He was pressed for explanations. That's what happens at a press conference; that's why it's *called* a press conference.

"For instance, one method of individual health care maintenance would be to watch the *New England Journal of Medicine* like a turtle watching a terrier. It goes ga-ga for cruciform vegetables; you go ga-ga for cruciform vegetables. It says, new hope for sausages; you go out and stock up on sausages. A lot of people live that way.

"In the Stopped Clock Lifestyle, you change nothing. That's the true implication of the Yo-Yo Effect: The Stopped Clock Lifestyle will be the optimally healthy lifestyle precisely as *often* as any other lifestyle. Not only that, every five years or so you'll find yourself on the cutting edge of medical research.

"My own real concern now is that *New England Journal of Medicine* will publish my findings. Then the Stopped Clock Lifestyle would become part of the Yo-Yo Effect, and that might be enough to break the tenuous fabric of reality entirely."

IN THE FORESTS OF THE NIGHT

Being the actual and complete testimony of David ben-Big, thoughtful journalist and free-lance social observer:

So I was up in this mountain cabin that we rented from these dentists, married couple, both dentists; they own homes everywhere. It's this good-fairy kind of thing: Put a diseased tooth under your pillow and you wake up in the morning and, poof, income property.

If I had a kid, I'd tell him, get braces and watch carefully. Ask questions. Learn a trade. Me, I do the prose-for-hire thing; I'm in commas; I'm commatose. Trade joke. I'd tell my kid, stay out of punctuation entirely.

So anyway, I am up in this mountain cabin. Clean air, clean water, pine needles, sunsets, no action whatsoever. So I have to make a fire. That's what you do in mountain cabins; you make a fire. Takes about seven hours. Then you go to bed. All night long, the fire rages. Wake up, it smells like ashes. For ashes and a toilet that doesn't work: $225 a weekend.

Fire is a seriously twisted kind of deal. You know how you hear on the news about how eight million acres of timberland were consumed by flames and the reporters ask "How did it happen?" and the spokesman always says: "Kids playing with matches."

So what do kids know that I don't? I got crumpled newspaper; I got kindling; I got small logs and medium logs and great behemoth logs you could kill elephants with.

What happens? I light the newspaper; nothing. I light the newspaper again; more nothing. I get more newspaper and crumple it and light it once again. Utter blackness and cold.

It's as if the fire knows. A two-year-old kid who doesn't know one end of a match from the other can burn an area the size of Cleveland; I can't get one sliver of kindling to burst into flame. We live in an evil universe.

This all relates to sperm. Don't laugh. The wife and me have been

175

trying. Like I said, we need a little dentist.

When I was growing up, sperm was the most powerful thing in the world; it was better than an atom bomb. I mean, you couldn't look at a girl without her delivering triplets on the spot. The shower; the swimming pool; separated by truck tires; didn't matter. The sperm would get there.

So now I'm married. It's all seriously legal. And what happened to old Mighty Tadpole, ceaseless impregnator of civilization? Not today, boss. My grandmother's funeral, boss. Have your people get back to my people.

I know what you're thinking. I had those tests. Polliwogs under the microscope. More potent than single malt Scotch; that's me.

So here's what I think: The fire and the sperm, they talk. They scheme. Only possible explanation. You take two of the most powerful forces on earth, questing beasts that will not be denied in any other situation, and suddenly they become the Indianapolis Colts of Primal Imperatives.

Collusion. That's the only answer. It was a done deal. The sperm knew somebody who knew somebody who knew the fire, and they had lunch in some oyster bar somewhere, and my life is all of a sudden cold and barren.

So I'm thinking and I'm thinking, and I suddenly realize: Maybe your primal forces don't like semicolons.

That's all I can figure. Tell your readers: Don't mess with sentence fragments. Full stops; that's the ticket. Whoops.

THE HUNT FOR RAINBOW BRITE

Magic Slate, a dime store toy created by a corset factory caretaker, has suddenly become the device du jour in counterintelligence. Representatives Dan Mica, D-Fla., and Olympia Snowe, R-Maine, used the pads for touring the bug-riddled U.S. Embassy in Moscow. . . . Others maintain that Etch-A-Sketch, although harder to write with, is a better spy buster.
—News Item

Britton Womb drained his glass of Sovietskiwasser and grimaced. "Tastes like kitchen cleanser," he said.

"The best of Gulag joy-juice," said Frank Hadley. He was slightly drunk. "Compounds designed to promote sterility and stupidity. You have secrets, comrade?"

"Not funny, Hadley," said Womb. He'd been at Moscow station only five months. "The walls have ears here at the embassy, you know."

"I wouldn't be surprised if the walls had an entire digestive system," said Hadley. Womb made a small noise in his throat. "Yessir, Mr. Womb. We proceed to plan two."

"We do," said Womb.

Hadley opened his briefcase and took out his Rainbow Brite Magic Slate. Womb reached under his chair and grabbed his Donald Duck Etch-A-Sketch.

"What's that?" asked Hadley.

"Etch-A-Sketch," said Womb. "Standard issue in D.C. these days. Sorry you don't have one."

"My old slate does me just fine," said Hadley.

Hadley raised an eyebrow at Womb. "Best to let me go first." He took the pointed stick and scrawled some words on the slate. Womb looked over his shoulder.

"What's that word?" asked Womb. "Nu Lear? Is that a business jet?"

"Nuclear," said Hadley. "The word is nuclear. There's a little wrinkle in the opaque paper. It gets like that."

"And here. There's some bubble or something. Miss Lyle? Is she mixed up with the Marines?"

"For Chrissakes, Britton, that's missile. Nuclear missile. Hold on; I can fix the bubble." There was a ripping noise.

"Now you've erased everything," said Womb.

"I know that," said Hadley.

Womb decided it was time to take charge. "Use my Etch-A-Sketch," he told Hadley. "State-of-the-art covert communications device. The president himself . . ."

"Anything you say, Womb," said Hadley. He grasped the two buttons at the bottom of the screen and began twirling. He worked feverishly for five minutes. Womb looked over his shoulder.

"Are," said Womb flatly. "Five minutes and you've given me three letters? A-R-E. Detroit could be thermonuclear toast before we finish this communication."

"Get with it, Womb. Remember the slate? Nuclear missiles are."

"Are what?"

"Give me a minute. You know what these damn things do to your hands? I've got double writer's cramp."

"There may be cameras," said Womb. "I'll just turn this over—"

"Noooooooo," screamed Hadley, but it was too late.

THE HYPNOTIC THRUM OF ELK SCAT

Among the many things that there is too much of in today's fast-paced world is nature writing. There is too much waxing poetic about the joys of creation. It tends to devalue the product; both products.

Don't get me wrong: I love nature. The wind, the snow, the little animals that burrow under your skin and eat your spleen; I love them all. But sometimes I swear to Vishnu if I read one more rhapsody on one more evening spent at the base of some damn mountain, I will cut down the first redwood tree I see and kill a whale with it.

Therefore, I have decided to create the world's first generic nature essay, suitable for all occasions; feel free to change the names and reprint at will. No charge; merely send me the pelt of a spotted owl:

It's morning in the Apronaski Mountains. The word apronaski means "land of the large naked women" in the Backho dialect of the Crow language. But large naked women no longer roam these ridges. Man the predator, man the pillager, has here as elsewhere destroyed the beings of great beauty, the eagle and the fox and the large naked woman.

I was up before dawn, listening to the hypnotic thrum of elk scat. In the lodgepole pine near my primitive camp, a squirrel squinted at the coming sunrise, its every sense alert. A hawk, every sense alert, swooped down and ate the squirrel.

That is nature raw, untamed, natural. It is a wildness beyond wildness, or a wildness to the right of wildness and in the next block. It is a wildness that man cannot understand, although I do.

The sky streaked vermillion as is its wont. The clouds, formed by layers of condensation from the rich slow breaths of the earth beneath the feet of deer and the robin, sprayed across the sky like clouds spraying across the sky.

Without seeming to know it, a great peace descends on my body. This is the time the Navaho call "mahrn'ning," the time when the goddess of the desert has congress with the god of the night. Their offspring, the "moolies," the offspring, ride in the orange chariot of the dawn, throwing small candies.

As Ralph Waldo Emerson once wrote, "Without the sky, the earth would be on top of us." I think of this as the sun reddens the dark tips of the mountains, and the saw grasses and fennel sweep their feathery fingers in the light morning breeze, waving farewell to yet another night, celebrating the return of what Gautama once called "pre-noon."

My journey is steep today. I must rise from my comfortable place and with every step move closer to the Beginning, the Trailhead, the start of the voyage, which is also its end. The small land frogs *(Froglocius bigii)* skitter down the sides of the vertiginous valley.

Are they saying, "Stay with us a little longer?" I do not think so. We are both children of nature; we understand that we each must go to our homes, to our burrows or our crummy motels in Bishop.

For there is a river beyond this river, and a river beyond that. My mouth drops open as I contemplate the consciousness of the river that is always beyond the river, the river that flowed before the first man set foot on this soft earth and will continue to flow long after the last man has gone, unless there is a drought.

As timeless as Brother Earth, I place my foot in front of my other foot, and on and on.

ANTIQUITY PERMEATES CHARMING LOGOUGH

After a week or two of touring a foreign country, you begin to suspect that you've read the same guidebook entry about 27 times. The names change, but the prose stays the same. That is the premise of this column, and a quaint 17th Century premise it is, too.

The picturesque market town of **Logough** is nestled between two hills (**Farmosh**, 570 m., and **Ratsnape**, 630 m.) on the south bank of the **River Quassie**. Local legend has it that St. Rodney of Tricot visited the town in 530 and converted at least two dozen lawn ornaments to Christianity. The spot of this historic event is marked by a small plaque and a large Holiday Inn, visible from the main road.

The **Logough Museum** (17 High Street, next to the Romanesque **Parish Church of Norman the Uncertain**) contains clothing and farm machinery dating from the early years of the 20th Century. Of particular interest is a pair of eyeglasses misplaced by Theodore Roosevelt, who visited the town unwillingly in 1906.

Ten kilometers north of Logough, on the road to **Sphere**, are the remains of the neolithic health spa, **Frim na Wacheet**. Some of the stones are literally thousands of years old, and scientists have found the remains of primitive Nautilus machines in the grassy mounds to the left of the largest circle.

Castle Logough (across the street from Sam Spud's Tater-To-Go) was entirely reconstructed in 1976. Tours leave from the car park every half-hour Mon-Sat May-Sept noon-5. The interesting collection of medieval torture devices was assembled in the 1940s by the 16th Earl of Watchbillie. The current Earl is dead.

Where to eat: **The Cottage** (102 Barren Crescent) is open for both lunch and dinner. Elf's Pocket, a local delicacy made from breaded organ meats and grain leavings, is the featured dish. After 9 p.m., local musicians gather in the foyer and steal valuable personal items from patrons.

The Logough Grill (36 Pathetic Mews) has an extensive selection of salted snacks and frozen sausages. The large shield above the fireplace was carried into the Battle of Rising Gorge (1761) by Wanda of Kent, and may be touched upon request.

Where to stay: Mrs. Louise Robertson presides over **Canal View Inn** just two blocks from Castle Logough. Her large friendly kitchen is a local gathering place, and many visitors have been entertained for literally minutes by the charming anecdotes told by long-time residents. Her eight rooms (some with beds) all have sinks, and three have fine views of the tallow works.

At **Hillock House** (13 Long Canings), Mrs. Armitage Shanks does everything she can to make her guests feel welcome. Her probing questions and ill-informed moral judgements make a stay at Hillock House a memorable one indeed. The low rates (@ 7 BNF) include a cold breakfast.

Logough after dark: **The Old Peacock** features traditional bean-dancing and cow-hurling every night except Monday. The atmosphere is informal and the mood infectious, with many first-time visitors joining in the circle-clap routine popularized in the motion picture *Alfie*. One warning: Guests are not permitted to leave the premises until they have eaten a pair of shoes.

HOW TO DRIVE IN INDONESIA

Here is an actual true fact you may wish to wrap in a handkerchief and put in your sock drawer until needed: If you drive like an American in Indonesia, you will die suddenly and completely.

To operate a motor vehicle in Indonesia, you must understand the transportation gestalt in an entirely different way. Definitions that you thought were above redefinition must immediately be redefined. Please pay attention.

• The Road: Includes not only the paved portion of the highway, but also what we might call "the verge," "the curb," "the sidewalk," "the front yard," "the roadside restaurant" and "the monastery." The paved portion of the roadway is generally one lane wide. Not one lane in each direction; one lane.

• Respect: All animals are granted the greatest respect in Indonesia. It is presumed that, being highly evolved creatures, chickens and dogs and other vertebrates know how to sidestep a Mitsubishi going 78 miles per hour on a fog-shrouded road during a national religious holiday. This same respect is granted to small children, cripples, men with 30 pounds of hay on their heads, unattended oxcarts and elderly women in mystic trances. Slowing or swerving to avoid these beings would cause them dishonor.

• Dishonor: Getting from morning to evening while remaining in the same incarnation.

• Lanes: These colorful white and yellow markings wish a hearty *Selamat datung* (Welcome!) to every traveler. They have no other function.

• Passing: The national sport of Indonesia. Observant motorists may encounter the vertical triple (passing three vehicles in one acceleratory movement), the horizontal triple (passing a vehicle that itself is in the process of passing a vehicle), or even the rare double-double (passing a vehicle at precisely the same time that another vehicle, coming in the other direction, is also engaged in the act of passing).

183

• Tailgating: What to do when not passing.

• Being passed: An insult not to be endured. The greater the difference between your vehicle (say, a broken tricycle) and the passing vehicle (say, a Boeing 747), the greater the potential loss of prestige. The owner of the less powerful vehicle must always do everything in his/her power to thwart the attempt to overtake.

• Seatbelts: Absolutely unnecessary. Not only are they not worn, they are not even provided. Passengers are fully protected by the horn (see below).

• Lights: Rapidly blinking the headlights can mean many things, including "OK to pass now," "dangerous to pass now," "get out of the way" or "may you find the thread of gold in the linen of existence." It takes years, sometimes entire lifetimes, to learn this subtle and intriguing intuitive nonverbal communication skill. Generally, however, you have about three seconds.

• The horn: When sounded loudly and frequently, the horn sets up an invisible energy barrier protecting the vehicle and its inhabitants from all harm. The faster the vehicle is going, the better the horn works. This is the central concept of Indonesian motoring.

• Accidents: Rare. Usually the result of a malfunctioning horn.

ARE WE ALL BOZOS ON THIS BOAT?

There was, Des Alwi assured us, no problem. Sometimes, it was true, the plane for Banda did not take off as scheduled. Sometimes the plane was overbooked. When you are a person in charge of a tropical paradise, you can only admit frankly that these things happen.

But there was no problem. His boat was, by sheer coincidence, leaving from Ambon for the overnight trip to Banda on the precise Friday in question. A stateroom was certain to be available. We would be welcome.

There would be a small charge. We understood. There was always a small charge. Breathe the air; see the sun; a small charge.

There would be no problem in finding the harbor. We should speak to his friend Mr. Nico. Mr. Nico was the assistant manager of the airport at Ambon. He would aid us in getting our passports expedited, in finding the harbor, in identifying the boat.

We located Mr. Nico on that fateful Friday. We were hot; we were tired; our garments were clinging damply to our flesh. Mr. Nico spoke a curious form of airport English.

"Mr. Jon and Mr. Jon's wife stand by Ambon town today," he told us. "Boat negative."

"Boat negative?"

"Stand by Ambon town harbor today. Not Garuda airline. Boat in Ambon town harbor."

We had not anticipated that Mr. Nico would accompany us in the taxicab. We had not anticipated that Mr. Nico would recapitulate events that had happened a mere 20 minutes earlier. "Mr. Jon arrive Ambon airport today," he remarked, more than once. Mr. Nico had very strong short-term memory skills; we had terrible short-term anticipation skills.

We arrived at Ambon town harbor, your basic sort of Lord Jim dock area. Sacks of rice; squads of disreputable young adults; sullen policemen; muttered curses. The smell of sewage floated in the air.

Mr. Nico bounded from the taxicab. "Affirmative Des Alwi boat!" he cried. There was only one boat at the dock. It appeared to have been constructed of rust and canvas. White paint hung in strips near the waterline. A goat stood near the prow, gazing suicidally at the water. Up the gangplank streamed a steady procession of people carrying rugs and tattered paper bags.

Had Lord Jim seen this vessel, he would have become a golf professional.

"Perhaps Des Alwi's boat is behind that boat," said my wife, hopefully.

"We are in very serious trouble here," I remarked.

Before we knew it, energetic young men were putting our luggage on board the S.S. American Nightmare. Simultaneously, a European couple were struggling off the ship.

"Bad stomach," said the man. "Perfectly safe, I'm sure. Just . . . I get seasick."

"So do I," said my wife.

"Mr. Nico stand by Ambon town Saturday!" yelled Mr. Nico.

My wife and I huddled. Our conversation was witnessed by 37 interested bystanders. "I'm not sure I want to be here," I said, watching our luggage being hurled into what appeared to be a storage locker but was in fact (we were to learn later) the aforementioned stateroom.

"Neither am I," said my wife.

That's when I really got scared. My wife is a person who thinks that danger is zany. My wife thinks that defying death is a really first-rate recreation.

If she's dubious, I'm comatose.

Our eyes met, as they have so many times before.

Simultaneously we decided that life was short, and if we perished at sea, ha ha ha to Shearson Lehman/American Express.

As Joseph Conrad once remarked.

NEEDLE POINT

So here I am, 2 in the afternoon on a rainy December Thursday, 30 miles from Quemado, New Mexico; 25 miles from the nearest paved road and 10 miles from the closest available human, in a cabin the size of a waterfront bar, all alone except for one black cat and 400 steel needles.

The needles are Art. The cat is Life, or anyway living. The cabin is Shelter, the cold chicken in the icebox is Food, and I am Man. There are a lot of abstractions out here on the lone prairie, a situation made all the more primal by the well-known absence of discouraging words.

The needles are out back behind the cabin. They are each about 20 feet tall and are set out in a grid 1 mile by 1 kilometer, 6 meters. They are pointed, like spears. They are regularly spaced, 220 feet apart, 16 on the kilometer side, 25 on the mile side. The tips of the poles are absolutely level, one with the other—a large sheet of glass placed on them would be supported at all 400 points.

The entire thing is called Lightning Field and is a permanent installation by Walter De Maria, an artist. People come from all over the world to see it.

Clearly, I should go see it too. I find some rubber boots in the closet—the ground is very muddy from last week's heavy snows and the subsequent thaw—and march out into the great flat prairie. The wind from the southwest is strong and cold. The light is flat and gray.

The cat follows me across the high desert plain, running ahead, waiting, meowing as I get close.

Half an hour later, I'm close to the center of the poles. I lean against one of them, my breath forming small puffs in the air, and squint down the lines. The needles march dutifully in all directions, eight ranks moving outward from my position.

I am supposed to be considering their relationship to nature, but I am distracted by nature itself. The clouds roll and tumble overhead. The snowcapped mountains on the horizon loom. I take an apple from my pocket and munch on it. My mind wanders through the corridors of memory—the Sierra and the Himalayas, the icy suburban streets of Illinois, eggnog, Dylan Thomas, late uncles, children.

Near sunset, a break in the clouds lets the low sunlight through. The tips of the poles glow faintly golden. Not bad. I don't know much about art, but I know what I like.

The coyotes begin to howl. I walk back to the cabin.

Much later, after dark, I stand in the kitchen of the cabin making myself another cup of Constant Comment—they're crazy for Constant Comment in the New Mexico highlands—and try to think about what I think. That cat is asleep under the Franklin stove in the next room. The wind whispers through the cracks in the walls.

I feel cozy and calm; I feel domestic. The poles outside are a long way away; what's central to my pleasure is the cabin itself. It's an amusing little dance of aesthetic opposites. The cabin is homey, sentimental, familiar, civilized; the poles are austere, intellectual, strange, arid.

Did Walter De Maria have this contrast in mind? Artists never say, of course; saying would be cheating. In the copy of *Artforum* that's been discreetly placed in the cabin, De Maria announces: "Isolation is the essence of Land Art." Who said it wasn't? Who even knows what Land Art is? The sky has miraculously cleared, and I go outside and stare at the Milky Way. I don't know much about astronomy, but I know what I like.

The next day, Mary the caretaker picks me up in her large blue truck. I ask her what she thinks about all these city folk driving to Quemado and bunking down at the cabin in order to spend 24 hours with these poles on the plains.

"They seem to like it," she says, in a voice that suggests that she has found the end of the conversation and it is here.

THREE RICE GRAINS ON MY FOREHEAD

It is the fashion question *Vogue* has refused to deal with: How do you accessorize a sarong when the plan for the day involves hiking up a volcano?

I was not entirely charmed by the notion of attempting to negotiate a 2500-foot elevation gain while wearing (let's face it) a dress, but I had no choice. We were to visit five Hindu shrines along the way and, in Bali at any rate, a sarong is required shrine attire. When in Rome and all that, although in Rome they do not climb mountains in evening gowns.

But a sarong covers a relatively small (although exquisitely important) part of the body; what should cover the rest of the body? I had been traveling for some weeks; my ensemble was, how you say, ad hoc and of necessity: an Oakland A's baseball hat, a Pickle Family Circus T-shirt, white socks and red tennis shoes.

In the cool morning air, this vision of multicultural oddness appeared in the mists of rice paddies, bowing and smiling to sundry Balinese agriculturists. "Nameste," it remarked, selecting a greeting from a nation half a dozen time zones away.

There was little work done in the valley that morning. There were prayers and drinking, I believe, but little work.

My outfit became, if anything, more eccentric as the hike up the mountain continued. A tropical volcano (even a semidormant one like Gunung Seraya) is frequently wreathed in clouds. Clouds mean moisture; moisture means mud. Bali has not yet achieved switchback technology. A trail up the mountain means a trail *up* the mountain. Mud was added to the fashion statement.

We were accompanied on our stroll into the lower reaches of heaven by three young Balinese men. They took turns carrying a large basket containing offerings to the gods. There were five temples along the way; that's a lot of offerings.

(It turned out that, after our offerings were blessed at the fifth temple, at the top of the mountain, the priest returned them to us. At that time, the offerings became "lunch." Hinduism is a very sensible religion.)

Naturally, the journey up the hill was impossibly lovely. Bali is one of those countries (New Zealand is the only other I've visited) that are so impossibly gorgeous that the landscape occasionally gives you the giggles. Not another series of terraced rice fields glowing golden in the morning light; not another sudden mountain towering over an azure sea; stop it, you're killing me.

Our guides for the trip were like 19-year-old guys anywhere, chatting up the girls along the trail, talking about their motorcycles, engaging in impromptu acts of physical competition. High spirited; polite; good kids.

And then we would reach a temple, and very matter of factly they would begin setting up for the ceremony, getting the holy water from the basket, finding the flower petals and rice grains, kneeling down in front of the high stone altar in the groves above the ocean and the fertile plains.

We were invited to kneel, too; the way to become a Hindu is to say "I'd like to become a Hindu." Time is not an issue; 10 minutes; forever; a prayer never hurts.

And we put the water to our lips, and we put the flower petals between our fingers, and we put three grains of rice on each of our foreheads, and we thought whatever thoughts we chose to think about God and trees and Bali, and that was it.

It was not like going to church; it was casual religion, worship as another normal event, like walking and flirting. Life is like that, most places.

BE KIND TO YOUR SMOOTH-BODIED FRIENDS

Think of playing catch. Think of taking a ball and glove and a friend and going out to the park and standing 15 yards apart and hurling the old spheroid.

What could be more pleasant? It's one of the oldest recreations in the world and still one of the most satisfying. You throw, I catch; then you throw, I catch. Sometimes I don't catch, so I run after the ball.

Usually I laugh as I run. In what other game is a mistake a cause for joy?

There are smaller games within the game. These games are unspoken, entirely internalized. Slowly, the two of us back up so that we are throwing at the comfortable limits of our ability to keep a ball airborne.

Then you lob one, and I circle under it. I do the same for you. Then one of us goes into a full pitcher's windup, and the other instinctively crouches like a catcher. Then we get silly and try to throw the ball behind our backs, or catch it between our legs.

Neither of us has to say, "let's get silly." We just do it. Unspoken communication.

And what I want to tell you is: That's what it's like to play games with a dolphin.

Recently I swam with the dolphins at the Steinhart Aquarium in San Francisco. It was an exhilarating, almost ecstatic experience, the best perk yet of the column gig.

The first impression is one of size. A dolphin is not a stuffed toy; it is one large, powerful muscle. Its ability to accelerate from a dead stop is astonishing. Thanks to years of brainwashing by Flipper and his friends, I was not afraid, although my peripheral nervous system was continually sending worried messages to my brain stem.

Are you sure this is a benign animal who wants only to help humans live in an ecologically sound biosphere? Sure looks like a big fish to us. Mammal? Tell us another one. . . .

When a dolphin sees a human in the water, it wants to play. No matter that the human doesn't know dolphin games; the dolphin will teach it.

The first dolphin game is called "Let's Touch The Dolphin." The dolphin lazes in the water waiting for the human to come closer. The human reaches out its hand, the dolphin flicks away. Human follows; dolphin waits. Reach, flick. Ha ha.

The next game is "Let's Get Dizzy." The human floats vertically in the water, treading slowly, peering through the mask. The dolphin circles the human. The human tries to follow; the dolphin circles more rapidly. Human fast, dolphin faster. When the human finally slows down, the dolphin scampers away.

The final game is "Chicken." The dolphin is at one end of the pool, the human at the other. The dolphin suddenly takes off, swimming straight toward the human. At the last moment, just before the disastrous collision, the dolphin veers away.

You can almost hear it laughing.

Look, I know the dolphin is yesterday's animal. Public attention has swung elsewhere, although I don't know where; maybe laboratory rats. But for the first time, in that tank at the Steinhart, I understood how seductive working with dolphins is, and how frustrating. The clichés demanded to be heard:

If only we could fully communicate, if only we could sit down over a nice plate of krill and talk about what we have discovered about the natural world and about each other, maybe even about the games we play. . . .

Hell, they already know how to play catch. If only we could teach them the infield fly rule.

THE JOYS OF AQUA-GLIDING

My theory about why everyone in the entire world does not snorkel has to do with the name: snorkel. If it were called aqua-gliding, everyone would do it. "Snorkel" sounds like hunting for truffles; it sounds like something your doctor would ask you to do if he wanted to check your sinuses.

"Just turn your head and snorkel for me, Mr. Carstairs."

It's a military word originally; a submariner's word. A sub snorkels more or less like a human snorkels; it glides along just under the water, taking in oxygen and disposing of noxious gases through long tubes.

Comes from the German *Schnorkel*, meaning air-intake. Schnorkel schnorkel schnorkel; just like the noises kids make on the playground to torture each other. Hardly a sport; more like the punchline of a grammar school joke.

But it is a sport, and a fine and wholesome one at that. It's also easy and cheap, and can only be done properly near a lovely tropical beach. That tends to upgrade the après-snorkel experience quite a bit.

Also, there are no snorkeling jerks, the way there are scuba jerks. Snorkeling and scuba are not the same thing at all, despite popular belief. Scuba (an acronym for Several Clambrains Underwater, Bizarrely Arrogant) involves tanks and valves and expensive synthetic body suits and little charts that tell you how many minutes you've got until your lungs explode.

Scuba also involves guys with knives strapped to their legs telling you about the time they were 180 feet down in the Marianas Trench when they noticed that a shark had severed their air hose so they had to make it to the surface carrying their wounded buddy through a colony of jellyfish, at night, during a rebel uprising, but no big deal heck they partied all night long afterwards.

In other words, people who make you feel that going down 40 feet and feeding the little fishies is pretty stupid.

Sometimes people who snorkel have to share boats with people

193

who scuba. Fortunately, the people who scuba soon fall off the boat, plunging into the depths in an activity that, in a very satisfactory way, resembles drowning.

People don't set records snorkeling; snorkelers don't hit the wall or feel the burn. Snorkelers paddle softly about with big floppy feet looking at the world under water.

On a coral reef, the world under water is endlessly surprising, alive with color and movement and light. It shifts under you as you shift over it.

The best part is the transition, the moment when your world changes from the long proximate horizon of water at eye level to the greenish liquid universe below, a place where gravity mutates and down is up.

Sometimes you shift worlds only to discover that you're in a previously unsuspected cloud of fish, thousands of silvery bodies turning and darting as one, so deft that you can float in the middle of them and not feel a single fin stroke.

Welcome to the planet that covers most of the earth.

TIDEPOOL TITANS

It was about 10 inches long, scarlet, shaped like a stout tongue depressor. She stood near the surf and held it aloft.

"Your basic chiton," she said.

I went over and looked at it. Its top, the side usually pointed toward the world, was hard and ridged. Its underside looked and felt like well-chilled tapioca pudding.

"Put it back," I said. "It can't be happy out here."

"Tidepool animals are used to being out of the water," she said. "That's the point of tidepools." But she kneeled anyway, pushed her sleeve above the elbow and dipped the chiton into the water.

Her plan had been to place it against the rock to which it had adhered before she had brought it sunward, but her foot slipped and her grip eased and the chiton floated to the bottom of the pool, belly up.

"What now?" I asked.

"We'll see," she said.

The chiton had fallen next to a sea anemone. A closed sea anemone looks more or less like a gray rubber ball stuck to a rock; an open anemone looks like an underwater flower. This one was closed tight—digesting, meditating, sleeping, something.

But it sensed the presence of Another. Slowly it unfolded, its blue-green tentacles expanding. It brushed the chiton, gently inquiring into the chiton's utility as a foodstuff. It was a big anemone, maybe seven inches in diameter. Both creatures were titans of the tidepool, where the average animal is smaller than your thumb.

While the anemone was engaged in its unhurried investigations, the chiton was trying to right itself. Its large orange-yellow foot stretched out and secured a purchase on a nearby rock. Then slowly—so slowly it was impossible to detect motion, possible only to detect change—it flipped itself over on top of the fully extended anemone.

And there it sat, a few stray blue-green tentacles visible under its

195

dull scarlet body. They had each, the chiton and the anemone, been trapped in the other's web; each had unwittingly delivered itself into the other's jaws. It was like a Mexican standoff, or a suicide pact.

"I wonder what chitons eat," she said.

"Nothing they have to chase," I said.

For a very long while, nothing whatsoever happened. A hermit crab busied itself on an opposite rock. A purple starfish, conscious of our shadows, moved deeper into its crevice. Behind us, sea palms waved and danced in the incoming tide.

Finally, though, the chiton snaked out its foot. It clutched the rock above it. The suckers, those tapioca spheres, stuck to the surface, and the chiton crept away from the anemone.

We watched for signs of the anemone uncovered in the wake of the sliding chiton, but we saw nothing.

"The chiton could not have eaten the anemone," I opined.

"Then where is it?" she asked.

A long time later, the anemone finally revealed itself. It had shut itself up completely, a tight flat mass of tissue almost invisible against the mottled gray of the rock. The chiton pulled itself along some more, and the anemone began to open up.

The anemone's tentacles floated again in the calm water. The chiton found a rock of suitable curvature and arranged itself. There they remained, thinking private thoughts.

What we had thought was a battle was merely a conversation without language. Two mutually inedible beings had negotiated their way out of a chance encounter.

Peace with honor was achieved.

SATURDAY NIGHT FIGHTS

I note that Ray (Boom Boom) Mancini is fighting again this weekend, and I am reminded of the one time I saw Mr. Mancini fight in person. He was in person and so was I. The venue was the Aladdin Hotel in Las Vegas; the opponent was a gentleman named Arturo Frias.

It was the first boxing match I had ever seen from ringside. I was present in my professional capacity, not to cover the fight but to cover someone who was covering the fight, a *Sports Illustrated* photographer named Andy Hayt. Since ringside seats were at a premium, and since the magazine I was working for, *American Photographer*, did not have a noticeable amount of clout in the boxing world, I was required to heft lenses, load cameras and generally carry on like an eager young *SI* assistant.

The fight was scheduled to start at 3 p.m., but at 8 in the morning the Mancini supporters were already lined up three deep at the bar, waving Italian flags, downing double bourbons and sporting T-shirts with the legend "I Love Youngstown," the Ohio steel-mill city that had spawned Mancini.

The day got hotter and drier, and the folks from Youngstown got hotter and wetter. By the time the doors opened at noon, the crowd had become entirely separated from its senses.

"Boom Boom, Boom Boom," they chanted.

After several preliminary bouts, the TV lights clicked on. The main event, 15 rounds of boxing for the lightweight champeenship of the world. Boom Boom, a pale, pockmarked young man with sly, nasty eyes, entered the ring first. He was followed by Frias, who looked very thin and very shy.

The crowd cheered the former and hurled abuse at the latter. The few Frias partisans attempted to express the opposite opinion. Large young men in yellow T-shirts roamed through the audience to make sure that the inevitable disagreements remained on a purely verbal level.

I squatted next to Hayt, ready to watch him photograph the fight.

Round One. Both fighters came out furiously, throwing dozens of punches in great blurry clusters and receiving a like number in return. Suddenly, only two minutes gone in the first round, Frias was in trouble. His hands went down and quivered by his sides. Mancini pressed the advantage. Frias fell, struggled to his feet. The referee peered into his strange, blank eyes and stopped the fight.

Behind me came an enormous roar. I looked around. A gigantic tsunami of people was bearing down on the ring. The bulky gentlemen in yellow T-shirts were bowled over by the wave. Chairs flew in the air like acrobats. I was conscious of one thing: These people all wanted to get into the ring, and one of the few things standing between them and their goal was. . . . me.

I was pushed and I was shoved, I was mauled and I was kidney punched, but the plucky magazine writer from California refused to hit the canvas. One man thrust a gigantic piece of cardboard into my arms. "Hold this," he said. I did until someone else knocked it out of my arms.

Twenty minutes later the guy came out of the ring. "Where's my goddam sign?" he began.

But the dominant memory from that afternoon does not involve Boom Boom or Frias or even Andy Hayt. It involves a large, aging black fighter who had taken the nickname Double Death. D.D. was fighting on the undercard; it is probably fair to say that he was a patsy, a tomato can, a fighter beyond his prime utilized to beef up the record of a younger opponent.

He came out gallantly, swaggering, glowering, bouncing waves of air off the wall with his looping right hands. But his opponent was swifter and smarter and younger, and D.D. got tagged pretty good on the chin in the third round. His eyes fluttered; one foot turned involuntarily inward; his shoulder twitched like the paw of a dreaming dog.

He fell heavily, slowly, sadly. His trunk hit the floor first, and then his head.

Boom.

Boom.

THE OLD GUYS IN THE PARKING LOT

Sometimes I can hardly see them at all. Their windows are up; the windshield reflects the trees, the skies, the big red Safeway S. They are like ghosts behind the glass, transparent, the scenery blending with their features.

They are waiting. They are not listening to the radio or running the air conditioner. To do so would deplete the battery, and I sense that these are men who worry about their batteries. They are not reading, perhaps because it is not easy to read on the driver's side; the steering wheel forces the arms up to the chest, so it's more like praying than reading.

They could get out and walk around the car and sit on the passenger's side and read, but that would feel foolish to them. A man should not be restless; a man should do his job. If his job is to wait, then he waits without complaint.

Or I think that's the idea. I am brimming with curiosity as I walk through the parking lot, catching glimpses of the old men in their cars, their heads bending toward their dashboards. Where do they buy those shirts, those paper-thin translucent white sports shirts with the huge armholes? I have never seen shirts like that in any store.

I want to know why they wear their hats in their cars. I want to know if they are filled with resentment or resignation or a great inner calm. I want to know what they think about as they wait in their cars with the windows rolled up on a nice spring day.

I have developed a whole narrative about these guys. They are waiting for their wives. They have driven their wives to the supermarket because their wives cannot drive themselves. Maybe their wives are sick, or their eyes are bad, or they just never learned to drive. The wives would be of that generation when many women just never bothered to learn.

Or maybe they drive because they always drive. Maybe they do only five things now, and one of them is drive.

But they do not shop. They are of that generation in which many men never learned to shop. They are impatient with shopping. They do not want to read labels. They do not want to mutter about the quality of produce. They hate coupons.

And so, having driven, they wait in their cars. They have always done it that way. It was not always such a big moment, the weekly shopping trip, but the other activities have fallen away, and now this is a capital O Outing, and they wait in the cars anyway, because they always have and because they fear the supermarket.

They grip their steering wheels, as though—I almost said, "as though at the edge of an abyss." But I do not know that. They're sitting in their cars; what the hell else are they supposed to do with their hands?

I have sometimes wanted to knock on the windows, to make tiny hand motions, to ask them what they were thinking about when I knocked. They would want to know why I asked, and I would not know what to say. Maybe: I'm interested in what happens to men when they get old. Could you tell me please about the oldness that you are now experiencing? Tell me about your wife now inside the market. Is she happy? Are you?

Do you ever long to go down the aisles with her, hand-in-hand? Do you talk on the way home? Do you ever say what was going through your mind, as you sat in your car with sky in your eyes running your thumbnail along the steering wheel? Is this the disease or the cure?

****

Readers will recall a recent column about the men (often older men in short-sleeve, semitransparent white shirts) who sit in cars in the parking lots of supermarkets, just waiting.

The column wondered who they were and why they waited. Several of them wrote in to explain. One was George Whitman of Alameda:

"My usual thoughts are of the Walter Mitty type in which I gently but firmly correct the tactical errors of General Schwarzkopf, the strategic mistakes of General Powell and the political miscues of Secretary Cheney. After accomplishing these, I deliver retroactive witty and crushing replies to all the supervisors, managers and other great and petty tyrants who have fired me, insulted me or snubbed me during the previous 70 years.

"I do not accompany my wife into the Safeway because I always pick up impractical foods such as squid, pigs' feet and sauerkraut in champagne sauce. My wife, whom I love dearly, gets exasperated when she sees such things in her shopping basket.

"At other times you may notice me in a sort of trance while I contemplate vast projects. For example, why do not soda crackers break on their perforations? They did when I was a boy. Now they merely shatter when touched, making mounds of crumbs.

"Occasionally, I may be pondering the state of my internal organs. The heart shudders now and then, the lungs plead for more oxygen, the brain demands more blood, the bladder seeks relief, the stomach needs fuel, and all the other messy things in there have their own methods of reminding me that I too am mortal.

"Am I happy? I really don't know. I have a nice home, a loving wife, a successful son, I've never been in jail, I tithe to my church, have served my country in two wars, and am relatively honest. I guess I am happy."

And as lovely as that is, it is not the only aspect of the old guys in the parking lot story. Betsy Day of Bancroft-Whitney publishing reminded me that some of the men-in-waiting are employed to do so.

"The old men in the Safeway lot are gypsy-cabbers. They ride us and our groceries home and courteously carry the bags to the porch. They are from Louisiana and Texas (the ones I know). Some are widowers. They bought their shirts there in the '40s and '50s.

"They seem fragile, outside it all, but somehow comfortable in their old-boy network."

The shadow economy; the filled need. Hooray for the old guys in the parking lot.

DIGGING OUT IN GUERNEVILLE

The first thing they don't tell you about the mud is that it's beauti-ful, a soft light brown. It looked like an inspired bit of interior design, a plush carpet of muted earth tones.

It even matched the dining room table, which was on top of the couch, which was on top of cinder blocks and boxes.

The second thing they don't tell you about the mud is how slippery it is. This isn't common yard mud; it's river silt, fine and slick, almost like butter. A stroll across the living room was an invitation to partici-pate in a Laurel and Hardy short.

That's where the mud was: in the living room. Also the kitchen, the bathroom, the study and the studio. All of those rooms (plus an upstairs bedroom and bath that emerged from the flood unscathed) belong to my friends Ray and Vel, who live 46 feet above the Russian River just outside of Guerneville.

The river crested late Monday at 49.5 feet; simple arithmetic yields an indoor water depth of 3.5 feet, sort of like the shallow end of a swimming pool. When the waters receded, the mud stayed behind.

A group of us went up on Saturday to help with the cleanup process. We stood in the hallway gazing at the devastation.

"Well," said Vel, "mi caca, su caca."

Volunteering to help a friend clean up after a flood is an extremely satisfying enterprise. It allows you to cloak a vulgar impulse to observe the picturesque chaos of disaster in the genteel garments of altruism.

We had driven slowly up River Road, rubbernecking like mad. Mailboxes in trees; garden hoses wrapped around the tops of bushes; a small frame house labeled "Office" wedged sideways between two red-wood trees; pathetic "For Sale" signs swinging in front of homes ripped from off their foundations.

The ham-fisted ironist of fate was everywhere evident. A car thickly coated with mud; in its rear window, a sign reading "Very clean; best offer." A mud-smeared sign next to a gigantic pile of roadside debris:

"No Littering."

In town, there was an almost manic atmosphere of good cheer. Any break in routine is something like a holiday. Guerneville is a town accustomed to floods; this one was unusual only in its severity.

The first problem in cleaning up after a flood is knowing where to start. Our little band, decked out in tattered clothing, holding mops and shovels and squeegees, looking like extras in one of those heart-rending Noble Farmer movies, stood on the back deck in solemn consultation.

"The rug definitely has to go," said Ray, "so maybe we should get all the furniture out of the living room and cut up the carpet."

"Where shall we put the furniture?" one of us asked. "In the side yard?"

"The side yard is knee-deep in junk," said Vel.

"Then let's clean up the side yard," said Ray.

Cleaning up the side yard involved a lot of decision-making. Was the barbecue ruined, or had they been planning to throw it out anyway? Is foam rubber salvageable? What about this soggy box containing Ray's aunt's menu collection?

"Being in a flood," said Ray, "forces you to come to grips with your possessions."

Finally we got the junk in the side yard sorted and pushed to the side. We moved inside and began to dismantle the rug. Easier typed than done: Even cut into smaller pieces, a water-logged rug is one of the heaviest things in creation. Gripping the rug firmly enough to carry it squishes the rug like a sponge; water leaks out the end in a broad stream. The entire process was like manhandling a waterfall through a Dutch door.

After the rug came the mud. Here's another true fact: There is no implement made that can adequately cope with fine, soft river-bottom mud. Mops, brooms, shovels and squeegees all have their drawbacks.

Particularly difficult is the mud in closets and underneath built-in furniture. "You'll have to use the notorious short-handled squeegee for that," said my friend Chuck.

"Not the short-handled squeegee!" I protested.

"I'm afraid so," said Chuck.

"Some day our people will be unionized," I told him. "Some day we will march through the town and make a bonfire with the notorious short-handled squeegees."

Chuck laughed. In fact, we all laughed a lot. It was hard work, but it was surprisingly pleasant. Ray and Vel felt good because we were helping with a long and tedious task; we felt good because (a) we were acting in the highest traditions of friendship and we knew it, and (b) we were getting exercise.

"The Russian River Diet Plan," said Ray.

Eventually dark came, and we stood around the deck drinking beer and talking.

"We were lucky," Vel said. "A lot of the expensive homes downstream at Northwood, across from the Bohemian Grove, were totally wiped out. Plus, we were on relatively high ground; plus, we have flood insurance."

Vel is a painter of Russian River scenes, mostly summer idylls, boaters and tubers and sunbathers skimming peacefully over the generous bosom of the river. Despite the mud and the flood, she retains her affection for the area.

"All this cleaning up is a drag, of course, but in a way, it's OK. The river does what the river wants to do. Sometimes we screw it up; sometimes it screws us up.

"Besides, maybe the flood will keep the developers away for a while."

DON'T TOUCH THAT DIAL

So there we were at the Odell Lake Lodge, wife and younger daughter and self, practicing sloth at the graduate level and watching the Cascades rise to obscure the sun.

We were having one of those rambling vacation conversations, filled with idle speculation and unexpected revelations. And my daughter said this: "When I have kids, I'm never going to let them watch television."

I knew the context: My daughter has recently become close with several members of a family that did indeed grow up without television.

Part of that had to do with happenstance—this family spent much time in a remote part of a foreign country—and part had to do with philosophy: The parents did not want television in the house, and somehow they made the resolution stick.

The house that my daughter grew up in (which is to say: my house) always had a television in it, at first because I wanted to watch it, later because it was such a convenient and inexpensive baby sitter/child distractor.

This other family is no happier than our family, its children neither more nor less passive. And yet I knew what my daughter meant. A life with television, when viewed in retrospect, inevitably seems a life with gaps. The gaps are holes in time; they can't be replaced.

And time is all a family has. Do you remember the trip you took when you were 11? Do you remember the plots of the television shows you watched when you were 11? Which seems more amusing now, more rewarding, more vivid?

So I had to agree: If I had to do it over again, I'd try to do it without television.

This has nothing to do with programming, nothing to do with the content of the shows. This is not one of those "Sesame Street" versus "Miami Vice" arguments.

I don't think there's too much sex and violence on television; there's probably too little. As an educational matter, fantasy violence should be real and scary, should be like violence itself; sex should be about love and pleasure, not about perfume and power.

That's what I want to teach my kids, anyway.

But this is not about content; this is about numbing out. This is about people stripped of both art and human contact; this is about people trapped in the most boring fantasy world imaginable.

There are some wonderful shows on television, but there's a better show sitting next to you on the couch.

That night, at Odell Lake Lodge, we went down to the big lodge room (roaring fire, books lining the walls, comfy battered couches) to play Uttar Pradesh, a card game we made up several years ago.

Because it's like a family secret, a game known only to us, playing it is a particularly rich form of communication, almost a private language. But there was a television on in the big lodge room.

We tried to sit at the other end of the room and play, but we could not. We could concentrate on the mechanics of play well enough, but the delight in tactics, the crosstalk and the groans, the sudden high cries of delight when an opponent was outwitted by guile, were gone.

The silences were filled; there was no room for us. Occasionally we would look up and lose the flow; whose turn is it? we would ask.

The roaring fire was too hot, the room was too stuffy. We didn't feel like playing anymore. We went upstairs singly, silently.

ALERT AND WATCHFUL, THE FIREMAN WAITED

Sarasota, Fla. (AP) - A World War II incendiary bomb washed ashore yesterday, and a firefighter was injured when it exploded after he hit it with an ax. — News item

The thing is: I know my job. All the way through training school, people said: Ed knows his job. I can enter a burning building. Most people cannot do that, but I can do that. I can enter a burning building.

And I can emerge. I can emerge from a burning building. Citizens often do not understand that that is the most important part of the job: emerging. Often I carry a small child when I emerge.

My face is caked with soot and sweat, my teeth look white and clean when I smile, when I smile down at the child who is looking at me with her eyes. Big eyes, usually. Often, she has poignant braces, the child.

I climb ladders well, hand over hand, as we were taught. Any other method is asking for it, as we said in rookie school. Thigh over thigh: Asking for it. I have a powerful two-hand ax stroke. I do the Dalmatian thing well.

In Sarasota, our Dalmatian is called "Domino," because of the spots. It sits up in front in the cab with its own hat, a red hat with a bill that swoops down in back, a hat that only firefighters and Dalmatians can wear. It's illegal for a citizen to wear that kind of hat; many people don't realize that.

When we get back from a fire, I cook up a passel of steaks with all the fixin's. Most of our food at the firehouse comes in passels, passels with fixin's. Then we play dominoes—the game, not the dog.

But there are parts of the job I don't like. Getting kittens down from trees; I don't like that. I'm a firefighter; I fight fires. Where's the fire with a kitten up a tree?

The first time I got one of those calls, I chopped down the tree. I used my two-hand grip. So, OK, I wasn't supposed to chop down the tree.

Got the darned kitten down safe and sound though. Took five minutes.

The other way takes hours.

And bicycle licenses. Where's the fire with a bicycle license? First time a kid came into the station for a license, I picked him up and emerged from the building. They said that was wrong, too, but the way he looked up at me . . . I'll tell ya, I just wished my face had been smeared with soot.

So last week we got the call about the incendiary device. I know incendiary means "fire," so this is real firefighter kind of work. Ed, they say, you're the man for this job.

So I put on my coat, the long brown coat with all the buckles. I put on my big black boots. I put on my gloves, big thick fire-resistant gloves. I pick up my ax. I walk out onto the beach.

It's darned hot on the beach, but I'm used to heat. The guys and gals in their bathing suits look at me as I walk across the beach. I'm walking tall and I'm walking proud; I'm one of Sarasota's finest.

I make up a little song as I walk: "He's walking tall, he's walking proud, say it loud, he's walking proud, he's a fire-fightin', fire-fightin', fire-fightin' GUY." I stand above the device, the device that threatens the citizens of Sarasota. I've been trained for this moment; I'm confident and relaxed.

I feel the muscles of my shoulders bunch under my heavy brown coat. I use my two-hand grip.

ALL DEPOSITS FULLY INSURED

The IRS has taken over management of the Mustang Ranch brothel near Reno, which is definitely an innovative concept for the revenue-strapped federal government. As always when new people are brought in at the top, things change. . . .

Scene: Mustang Ranch, a federally managed brothel. A customer, having waited in line for 20 minutes, approaches the Formica counter that runs the length of the office. A sign behind the counter reads: "United States Department of Sexual Resources Management."

Customer: I'd like the, you know. . . .

Clerk: Sexual services?

Customer: Yes, that would be the . . . what I want thing.

Clerk: Regular or fantasy?

Customer: I suppose, well, fantasy sounds nice.

Clerk: Night nurse, flight attendant, Swedish mountain climber, scullery maid or United States senator?

Customer: United States senator?

Clerk: Look, mister, I don't write the rules; I just follow 'em. Do you know we're being sued by the Libertarians because they're not an option? And the senator fantasy is not exactly a profit center around here, if you take my meaning. But, hey, you can't fight Capitol Hill.

Customer: I guess not. Well, maybe I'll take the night nurse.

Clerk: You and half of America. OK, take this form to Window Six.

The customer shuffles down the counter to another line. He waits for another 20 minutes. He passes the time by reading a pamphlet titled "Safety in the Sexual Workplace." He learns a great deal about proper lubricant disposal.

Finally, it's his turn at Window Six.

Customer: Is this for the nurse thing?

Clerk: I need you to read the pink form and initial it at the red X's, please, here and here and here and here. I need you to fill out the green form except for questions 12 to 15, which are now illegal. Look at the card behind me and read the second line.

Customer: Vlerkmurph.

Clerk: Ha ha. This is an eye test, friend. Read the letters.

Customer: Why do I need an eye test for the, uh, night nurse?

Clerk: I don't make the laws, fella, I just follow 'em. Read the chart.

Customer: V L R K M R F.

Clerk: Congratulations, you're not blind. When you've completed the form, follow the yellow line on the floor to Room D as in dog. Got it?

Customer: Sure.

The customer fills out the form, which includes a pledge not to reveal confidential information "while in the grip of orgasmic response." He takes the form, follows the yellow line and arrives at Room D.

There are perhaps 50 other men in the room, all sitting in gray folding chairs. Some are smoking. Posted on the bulletin board near the door is a flyer reading: "Sex is fun. Enjoy yourself!"

A man in a USDSRM uniform walks in. "Sorry for the delay, men. I'm just here to tell you that the women you are about to meet are not actual nurses and, should you experience any medical emergency, please seek help from a qualified physician or health-care specialist. On behalf of all of us here at Mustang Ranch, I'd like to thank you for choosing the federal government, where we've been screwing citizens since 1776."